STORM
CAT

STORM CAT

Margi McAllister

SCHOLASTIC

Scholastic Children's Books
An imprint of Scholastic Ltd
Euston House, 24 Eversholt Street, London, NW1 1DB, UK
Registered office: Westfield Road, Southam, Warwickshire, CV47 0RA

SCHOLASTIC and associated logos are trademarks and/or
registered trademarks of Scholastic Inc.

First published in the UK by Scholastic Ltd, 2016

ISBN 978 1407 16522 6

A CIP catalogue record for this book
is available from the British Library.

Printed by CPI Group (UK) Ltd, Croydon, CR0 4YY

Papers used by Scholastic Children's Books are made
from wood grown in sustainable forests.

1 3 5 7 9 10 8 6 4 2

This is a work of fiction. Names, characters, places, incidents
and dialogues are products of the author's imagination or are used
fictitiously. Any resemblance to actual people, living or dead,
events or locales is entirely coincidental.

www.scholastic.co.uk

For Helen Hay

Chapter One

What do you think of when someone says "winter"? Christmas? Snowball fights? If you think of rain and dark nights you're probably English (and a bit of a misery, to be honest). If you think of solid ice, bitter cold and bears roaming about you might be Canadian – or come to think of it, Narnian.

A year ago, I found a whole new kind of winter.

Libby Sutton. Fifteen.
Loves: animals, books and lemon bonbons.
Hates: bullying, spitefulness and tuna fish.

A year ago I was fourteen, and so far everything was all right. Well, sort of all right. As all right as it needed to be. There were two of us at home, me and my mum –

her name's Kate and she's an outstanding photographer. Mostly she photographs places, especially landscapes. My dad scarpered off to the States when I was very little and turns up now and again, but never for long. He's the "clever but clueless" type. That's all you need to know about him.

Mum does freelance work for advertising and displays and all that sort of thing, so she often has to work away from home. When that happens I stay with my grandparents. I am *so* lucky to have them. Granny and Grandpa's house is only ten minutes walk from home, and possibly my favourite place in the world, the place where I've always felt right. I feel I'm more myself there than anywhere else, even at home. That's where I learned about animals, and especially wild ones, because Granny and Grandpa volunteer with an animal rescue charity. As soon as I could walk I was helping them to rescue toads and hedgehogs. There are horses and ponies in a field behind their house, and they've got Poppy. She's a shaggy old mongrel from a rescue centre. Poppy's so ancient that I'm sending for her bus pass and a birthday card from the Queen, but she just keeps going. When I'm there, Poppy and I we go for long walks together and she sleeps on my bed, and nobody minds. I help with the horses, too, and when Granny and Grandpa saw how much I enjoyed it they gave me riding lessons for my birthday. They're like that. They understand.

THE LIBBY SUTTON VERY (VERY) BASIC GUIDE TO WILDLIFE:

If a hedgehog is out in daylight, it shouldn't be. Observe it. It's probably ill, and needs the vet.

Always leave clean water out.

If it's small and chubby with a short tail, it's probably a vole.

If it's small with a pointy nose, it's probably a shrew.

If it's small and wears glasses, it might be my granny. Give her a hug from me.

We used to have family holidays all together, and none of us wanted to get hot and sticky on crowded foreign beaches. We'd go to the New Forest where donkeys wander about in the streets and there are deer and wild ponies, or the Lake District to watch red squirrels.

Mum and I have always been close. Sometimes we'd get on each other's nerves, but mostly it was good. Now and again she'd date somebody, but it never lasted long. There was never anybody who looked like being "the one" – nobody she wanted me to meet. And then at last she started telling me about Gray.

Gray, she told me, was short for Graham, and they

met when they were both working on an advertising project in the Scottish Borders. They worked together a lot after that, and I could tell from the way she talked that she thought Gray might be The Real Thing. He was a widower with a six-year-old son, Cam – short for Cameron. (What is wrong with these people, can't they remember their own names?) It gets a bit embarrassing when your mum comes home like a soppy teenager going on about her boyfriend, but in another way it was sweet. Gray was clever and kind, she said, and fun to be with. Then she'd shrug and smile, and say, "and Cam's such a funny little thing." She said it kindly, and I wondered what she meant.

Somewhere along the way, I got an uneasy feeling about this. She talked more and more about Gray and he sounded too good to be true. Mum deserves a medal for coping so well on her own and achieving so much. She's a cool, clever woman with style. She always looks great even in jeans and an old sweater, and she's famously good at her job. She's kind of glossy, if you know what I mean. But sometimes, clever people can be hopeless about obvious things, like "who to fall in love with". She fell for my clever-but-clueless dad, didn't she? And look what happened there. I didn't want her to get hurt again.

For months, she went on about Gray and "funny little Cam". She always said Cam was "odd" or "funny". What was so funny about him? Funny ha-ha or funny peculiar? Did he have three legs? A tail? Horns? At full moon, did he turn into a boggart? But Cam's mum

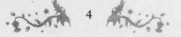

had died of cancer when he was three and a half. Poor kid. That must be the worst thing that can happen to a child. It wasn't surprising if he was a bit "funny".

Just after Christmas Mum had to go away on an assignment and I had an extra-long stay with Granny and Grandpa. I took Poppy for long walks, but she couldn't understand why there weren't any rabbits to chase. It was bitterly cold, and any rabbit with half a brain would be down the burrow wrapped in its duvet eating choccies and catching up on the Christmas telly, but Poppy couldn't get her head around that. Anyway, as soon as Mum got home and we were both back in our own kitchen, she made hot chocolate and sat down opposite me at the table. I remember thinking how different we were, Mum small and dark and smooth in tight black trousers and a sweater, and me with long mad hair, wearing the first thing that dropped out of the wardrobe when I got in from school.

"I've got something exciting to tell you," she said, looking at me over the top of her mug. "Gray and I have been talking. We think it would be a good idea if we all met up."

Thank goodness for that. I'd been afraid she was going to say they were getting married, and I hadn't checked him out yet.

"You know I'm fond of Gray," she said. "He's a big part of my life. But we need to see how we all get on, so we'd like to get us all together at half term."

"Are they coming to stay here?" I asked. It would be a tight squeeze, but we'd cope.

"No, we thought we should meet on neutral ground," said Mum. "Not in our home, and not in theirs. So we're all going away together. We've booked a cottage in Scotland, way up in the Highlands. It's a long drive, and we'll meet Gray and Cam there."

The Highlands? Wow, that was a first. We'd been to Scotland before, but no further north than Edinburgh and that's not very far north at all. (By the way if your geography's rubbish, north is up, and Scotland is the wiggly bit at the top of the map.) I'd never been to the Highlands. It's a popular place for skiing, which Mum used to do a long time ago, but she hadn't been to a ski slope for years and years. She took me once, when I was very little. I can remember two things about it. One is my cute little red snowsuit (wasn't I sweet?) and the other is bellowing blue-black-purple murder because these people wanted me to slide down a sheet of solid ice. I still can't see the point of skiing. It's understandable if you live on the top of a mountain and you need to get somewhere urgently, yes, but to do that for fun?

Anyway, there was more than skiing in the Highlands. It's the most fantastic place for wildlife. You can see those pretty red squirrels up there, and there are deer, and eagles, and fat little birds called ptarmigan, and those tough shaggy little ponies. I could go for that.

I found the postcode for the cottage and looked it up on that website that lets you see places. There was a mountain, a lot of moorland all around it, a forest and a squat grey thing. The squat grey thing was the cottage we'd be sharing with Gray the Totally Wonderful and Funny Little Cam. If it didn't work out, well, at least it was only a few days, and it would take most of the first one getting there.

So – Mum and I left on the Saturday morning and after three hours and a coffee stop I could see all around that we were in a different country. The landscapes were grim, rough and magical all at the same time, and in spite of the rising hills with their little silvery waterfalls there was so much sky! I'd been texting, but I put my phone away because I didn't want to miss any of it and anyway the signal kept dropping in and out. As we drove further north the sky grew silvery-grey like pewter and by the time we turned off the main road there were light flakes of snow drifting around us. Mountains in the distance were streaked with white.

The further we drove, the more the snow swirled round us. Forget the Christmas cards. This was the real thing, and it didn't stop.

Snow brings its own kind of quiet. I turned off my music because it seemed wrong to listen to it here. There was the steady whirr of the engine and occasionally the harsh call of a bird or the gurgle of a stream, but those sounds stood out starkly against the background of silence. Snow was settling on harsh rocks with rough silvery lichen and on grey-green moorland. When I was a little kid and we went driving in the snow I used to pretend that the car was a magic carriage flying through the air. I don't mind telling you, in that enchantment of snow, moor and mountains I did it again.

"Mum!" I gasped suddenly, and pointed. I wished I hadn't because she jumped and her foot slipped, but she kept control of the car and slowed down.

"What?" she said a bit crossly.

"It's a hare," I whispered. I had to point it out to her because only the black tips of its ears stood out against the white – and I had to whisper because the snowy moors and the sight of the hare, with its ears that looked too big for it and its long legs, nearly left me speechless. It had a strange, wild look about it. People used to think that hares were magic. Looking at this one, I could almost believe it. He turned and leapt away on those long, powerful paws.

"Wow!" I said, and I felt that whatever happened on this holiday would be worth it because I'd seen the wild, white, gangly hare. But I hadn't yet learned what the hare had to teach me. The Highlands have their own rules.

In that short time the snow had been getting heavier. Mum drove steadily, cautiously. I knew she wanted to reach the cottage while she could still get through, but it wasn't easy. In the last half hour we'd only seen one other car and Mum had had to pull over to let it through because the road was so narrow. She was glancing at the clock, and I knew she wanted to be there before dark.

"I hope Gray and Cam make it all right," she said. I nearly said, "they'll be fine," but by this time I could

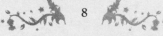

hardly see green and grey around us any more, only white. Snow had settled on the pine trees. I began to wonder what it would be like to be stranded.

Imagine. You're driving through the snow until you can't see ahead; you have to crawl, slower and slower, until you stop altogether. It's still snowing, drifting all around you. Darkness settles, *real* darkness. No street lights. You might have a torch or a light on your phone, and that's all. At first it would be exciting, like an adventure. You'd huddle up together and if you had a smartphone or some kind of e-reader you could read. But it would grow colder and colder, you'd be hungry and thirsty. You'd have whatever you came with, no more. No hot drinks. Maybe a rug in the boot to wrap up in. All you could do would be to wait for morning, but that might seem like for ever. *Imagine*.

I said it anyway. "They'll be fine, Mum."

There was still no house in sight. Through the falling snow I could make out a grey glaze of ice on water, and then it wasn't a road at all, just a rocky, bumpy track – then finally, round the corner was the plainest, greyest square of a house I'd ever seen. It was nothing to look at – there was almost more snow than roof – but in the windows was the warm light that means somebody's in. A splashed old Land Rover was parked outside with a collie dog in it, and that couldn't possibly belong to Gorgeous Gray.

"This is us," said Mum. She parked the car, slumped back in her seat and sighed, and I realized what a hard drive it had been for her. Then the front door opened, and in the light from the doorway stood a dumpy, smiling, grey-haired woman in a thick woolly skirt and sweater. As I opened the door she called out to us.

"Kate and Libby Sutton? Come in out of the snow! It's toasty warm in here and the kettle's on!"

We climbed stiffly out of the car, stretched our legs and waded through snowdrifts to the door. The warmth of the house wrapped me up and the woman's soft Scottish accent was full of kindness.

"I'm the owner, Ailsa Chisholm," she said. "Welcome to a real Highland winter!"

She ushered us into a room of big, soft settees and chairs, a rather ugly sideboard, an old-fashioned dining-room table pushed against the wall, and, best of all, a real fire flaring and crackling in the grate with a smell of wood smoke that reminded me of Granny and Grandpa's house. I felt so at home! I could have happily curled up on the rag rug by the hearth and just stared into the fire like a cat, but Ailsa was showing us the house. The kitchen and bathroom were simple and modern, like in a normal house, which in a way was a bit disappointing, but the bedrooms made up for it. There were two, each with two single beds, patchwork quilts, and low windows looking out over the snow. I liked the front bedroom best as it had windows on two sides. If I could have the bed on the left I could roll over in bed and look out of the low window with its white painted frame and flowery old-fashioned curtains.

"This one's ours," I said firmly. I planted my handbag

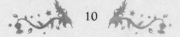

on the bed I wanted and Mum's on the other to make it perfectly clear who slept where, and then crouched down to look outside.

"There's a pony in the snow!" I said. There she was: a little grey pony, short and shaggy with a long thick mane and a rug over her back. What a little sweetie! She stood patiently, one hoof tilted, her head down against the storm.

"That's our wee Peggy," said Ailsa. "Peggy the pony. She's a real Highlander, as tough as the heather. You might not be able to see Jayjay from there; he's the donkey. He usually stands on the other side of her."

"Aren't they freezing?" I asked.

"They're hardy old things," Ailsa told me, "and there's a shed for them at the other end of the field, but you can't see it from here. I live just half a mile along the track with my husband and my son when he's home, and one of us comes down each morning to turn them out and each evening to bring them in." She went on to explain about how everything in the house worked, and finally said, "The directions to my house are on the fridge door, should you need them. The phone number is there too, but mind, mobile phones are not reliable round here. There's a landline, but that only takes incoming calls; you can't dial out from it. Now, while I'm here, I'll put Peggy and Jayjay inside."

"Can I help?" I asked quickly. "I help with the ponies near my granny's house."

She looked surprised. "Don't you want to stay here in the warm?"

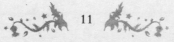

"I don't mind!" I said. I wanted to meet Peggy and Jayjay, and it's all right getting soaking wet and cold when you can come back to a real fire. Mum kept looking out of the window and I knew she was watching for Gray and Cam and hoping they weren't stuck in a snowdrift. I got my wellies on, took an apple from the car – we'd brought tons of them – and went out with Ailsa.

The snow had settled where it fell, and lay in heaps on the bushes. Even the sky was white. Jayjay had a bonnet of snow between his ears until he gave himself a good shake and it sprayed around him. I bit into the apple so I could pull off chunks of it for Jayjay and Peggy and they stood chewing and slavering while I patted their warm necks and stroked their thick winter coats. They twitched their ears and nudged me for more apple, and when Ailsa came with the lead ropes to take them to the shed, they didn't need much persuading. Hey, this was my kind of holiday! I'd only just arrived and I was stabling a pony!

The shed smelt of hay and horses, and we brushed Peggy and Jayjay until a snowstorm of grey hairs floated around us, and we coughed and laughed at the same time. It made us friends. We strung up nets of hay, and if I tell you that the smell made me feel empty with hunger, don't misunderstand me; I don't eat hay. It just smelt good enough to eat, and I realized I was starving. Peggy and Jayjay huffed and snorted and stamped, and pulled hay down from the nets. We filled the water buckets at an outside tap, and by the time we'd finished there was a touch of pale gold and pink in the sky. We still had a little time before dark. I'd been thinking about going inside and warming my frozen hands at the fire, *but* – you're never too old to build a snowman.

Earlier the drifted snow had looked too beautiful to spoil, draped across the grass like fur around a queen's shoulders, but it was too late now. Ailsa and I had already crossed it in our stomping great wellies and we'd be doing that again, so I pitched in and Ailsa helped me to get started. By the time she plodded back to her Land Rover we'd made a fat, round snowman body, but a Headless Snowman is not a Happy Snowman, and besides, he looked spooky. I rolled him a head, found some sticks for arms, and, after a bit of digging about in the snow, had enough pebbles for his eyes and a smile.

Once his face was on, with his big smile, that snowman had personality. Not much of an IQ, but personality. Mum looked out and I waved, and I could see that she was pleased I was having fun like a little kid. *Good.* That would stop her from worrying about Gray and Cam. I took a picture of my snowman. I wished I'd put his face on the other side, then I could roll over in bed in the morning and see him grinning inanely back at me, telling me to get up. This was going to be fun. He'd be there to welcome little Cam. Whatever was funny about that kid, he was sure to like snowmen, because all kids do. If it stayed as cold as this it would last the whole holiday and be our snow mascot. Perhaps Funny Little Cam would like to give it a name.

All that the snowman needed was a hat and scarf. I was just heading back to the house to see what I could find when I heard an engine, and soon there was the glow of headlights on the snow. In no time Mum was on the doorstep, and as the car drove up I could see a tallish man with short curly hair and a small boy sitting beside him.

The car was one of those big hunky four-wheel-drive things, half chariot, half tractor. And on the roof there were – *oh no, this doesn't look good* – skis. I should have thought of that. *Mountains, winter. No-brainer*.

Gray parked outside the cottage and, with a banging of doors, the two of them got out. Gray was much as I'd expected – tall, gingery-brown hair, quite nice-looking in a way that would appeal to someone old enough to have a fourteen-year-old daughter. Cam was smoothly black-haired and his eyes so big and dark that I thought of a snowman, with coals for eyes. There was something else about Cam's eyes. I saw it and it bothered me, but at the time I didn't know what it was. By the end of the holiday I did.

Gray and Mum exchanged a quick kiss, a bit awkwardly as if they had to behave themselves in front of Cam and me, but Cam ignored them. He was clutching a cuddly black dog which he suddenly threw into the air and caught again. He repeated this over and over. Sometimes he caught it; sometimes it landed in the snow. Then, solemnly, he put his feet together, jumped, and looked astonished that he hadn't fallen down a rabbit hole. As Gray got their cases out of the car, quite suddenly, Cam gave a roar like the battle cry of a raging bull elephant. He charged full tilt at my snowman, bulldozed it, kicked it, and jumped up and down on what was left.

Well, what a little poppet. What a lovely time we'd have if I managed not to throttle him. . .

And Gray? He saw it all and didn't say a thing.

Chapter Two

Boys will be boys, I thought, and just laughed about it, because wasn't I far too old to get into a huff about a knocked-down snowman? We all went indoors, but only after Cam had stopped on the doorstep with an imaginary gun and powered-off a few rounds into the hall while shouting, "Ack-ack-ack-ack-ack-ack-ack!" Oh, joy. The noise was painful. That was when I found out about Cam's volume control, and that it didn't work. Once he'd finished *ack-acking* he ran into the first bedroom he came to, which was mine and Mum's.

"This way, Cam!" said Gray, and he waited in the doorway while Funny Little Cam fired his imaginary gun out of both windows, and honestly, I think a real machine gun would have been quieter. Then he went round every room in turn sniping out of the windows, nodded at his father as if to announce "job done" and then went back to look at his bedroom. He must have decided he liked it, because he took his little backpack and emptied it on to the floor. He had what I recognized as the latest tablet computer (he was six, for goodness' sake) three teddies and a cuddly rabbit. I thought that was strange. Five cuddly toys, including the black dog. I know that little boys still like teddies, but they don't usually want anyone to know about it. He lined them all up on one of the beds then turned to me and said, "You can't touch them."

"Oh, Cam!" said Gray gently, "That's not very—"

"That's fine, Cam," I said with a smile, because I had to be really grown-up about this, didn't I? "I won't touch them."

I don't think he believed me, because he glared in my direction. Oh, wasn't it all going terribly well! He rearranged the teddies and sat on the floor with the tablet, and Gray wandered off to the kitchen. Mum had already started to cook. It was just something out of tins and packets, but it smelt good.

"Kate, I'm going to take a look around outside while there's still any light left," said Gray. "I need to stretch my legs."

I was a bit surprised. He should have stayed with Cam, and he hadn't even offered to help in the kitchen. But no, he put on a hat – it was one of those daft Russian things like a curly black cat, and I had to rush out of the way before I started giggling – and strode out like an Arctic explorer. Cam scowled down at the screen, and I went to the kitchen to help Mum. When the rush of cold air nearly knocked me flat I realized that Gray had left the door open.

Honestly and truly, I wanted to like Gray for Mum's sake. I wanted him to make her happy. But for that very reason he had to be good enough, and my standards for Mum were high. In my head I had a checklist, and it was going like this:

GRAY
- Gives six-year-old a fancy new tablet.
- Allows said six-year-old to do whatever he likes (too loudly) then pushes off leaving:
  (a) Mum to cook
  (b) me to mind the moppet
  (c) the front door open.

Oh, dear.

When we'd first talked about this holiday I'd sort of guessed that I'd end up being Chief Minder of the Moppet. I just hadn't expected it to happen this soon, or for Cam to be such a brat. Thinking of Cam I decided to check on him – I'd left him in a room with a fire, for heaven's sake, and he was capable of moving the fireguard if he felt like it – but then he trotted into the kitchen with his black dog in his arm and settled himself down on a stool, watching Mum. And that was that. From then on his eyes were fixed on her, following her, watching her hands as she put the plates in the oven to warm. The kitchen was so tiny that it was crowded with three of us in there.

"You must be starving, Cam," said Mum. She must have felt his eyes on her, like when a dog watches you eat, but he didn't look hungry, exactly. He just looked as if he wanted to eat Mum. I left them there and laid the table in the sitting room. The fire had gone down a bit, but it was crackling away to itself just the way a real fire should.

Just as Mum said that tea was about to be served and sent Cam to wash, there was a banging at the door. Gray's stomach must have told him that the food was ready and, *oops,* I'd locked him outside in six inches of Siberian winter. What with the snow on his shoulders, his silly hat and his nose red with the cold, I thought he might burst into "We Wish You A Merry Christmas". He came in and stamped snow off his boots.

"It's amazing out there!" he said. "It's beautiful: the dark is really, really dark, and..." and he yabbered on about snow and moonlight and rechargeable torch batteries and "let's all go out for a walk this evening". *Let's not,* I thought, but thank goodness, Mum herded everyone to the table and Cam plonked himself firmly down next to her. He didn't say much, but Gray talked enough for both of them.

"We meant to get here loads earlier," he said. "We planned to arrive before you so we'd have the fires lit and the kettle on, but we had to stop a lot on the way, didn't we, Cam?"

Cam frowned down at his plate. "We had to stop a lot," he repeated. "Dad took photographs."

As you do, I thought. You're driving through the far end of nowhere in a blizzard with a small child in the car, so instead of heading for the nearest four walls and a roof you get out and take photographs.

"The lady who owns the house was here to meet us," I said. "Ailsa. She had the fire going and everything. It was lovely and cosy for us." I said it with a nice smile, but what I meant was *Don't worry, it didn't matter whether you were here or not.* We'd brought cake for afters, and Cam cut his very neatly into tiny pieces and ate them slowly, one little square at a time as if he wanted to make it last for ever. Before we'd finished Gray was up from the table and hunting through the cupboards like a Labrador looking for a ball.

"Found them!" he announced gleefully. He stood up clutching a handful of leaflets and brochures about places to visit, the kind of thing you get in tourist information centres. "They always have some of these in holiday places."

He dropped the leaflets on to the middle of the table. (I moved the cake in time.) They were about all the local attractions and there were lots of them, especially considering that we were twenty miles from civilization. As well as what-jolly-fun skiing there were hill walks, a wildlife centre, a buy-your-own-tartan place with a museum, pony trekking, art galleries, and a pottery. (Wherever you go on holiday, there's always an art gallery and a pottery.) Gray was going through them all and handing them round – "That looks good – oh, it's closed until April. Cam, there's an animal place – and a sculpture gallery, do you fancy that, Kate?" Cam drew circles on his plate with a sticky finger.

"What about you, Libby?" asked Gray. "There's pony trekking, if you're into that."

I do love pony trekking, but in three feet of snow? Do they make thermal knickers for ponies? I was pretty certain there wouldn't be anything happening on the pony trekking front. But there was something I wanted to do – he could bet his silly Russian hat there was. I longed to go to that sweet little bedroom, curl up with a duvet and a book, and have the space all to myself, with just a bedside lamp and the snow falling outside the window. And I wanted Gray to stop being so bouncy and enthusiastic. Couldn't he just shut up and eat cake? At least he'd forgotten his idea about a moonlight walk. If he'd understood much about remote places he would have realized that moonlight isn't a lot of use in a landscape you don't have a clue about.

"I don't mind," I said. Cam had already got down from the table without asking and without Gray noticing, and was walking round in circles with his black dog under his arm. Finally he sat down by the fire.

"Have we got wifi?" he asked.

"I wouldn't think so," said Gray. "Especially in this weather."

Give me strength. Where do they think they are? Do the sheep have broadband?

21

Cam scowled, fiddled about with the tablet, then suddenly flung it on to the settee, ran at the wall, kicked it and yelled as if he'd been bitten by a werewolf. He had shoes on and couldn't kick very hard, and the yell sounded a bit stagey to me. Mum and Gray must have thought so too, because they let him get on with it. When he realized he wasn't getting any sympathy he stopped yelling and curled himself into a grumpy little bundle of sulks on the settee. Gray suddenly stopped shuffling leaflets about and got up.

"It's getting cold," he said. The fire had died down to a gentle glow, and Gray heaved half a tree trunk from the log basket. I was used to open fires and he clearly wasn't. I could see what would happen, so I jumped up.

"Shall I do that?" I offered, but I was too late. Gray dropped the chunk of wood on the fire.

Whoosh! Sparks flew up the chimney and on to the rug, hot ashes rose into the air, clouds of grey smoke billowed out into the room. Gray shot away backwards, and there was a smell a bit like roast pork because he'd singed the hairs on the back of his hands. Cam shrieked like a siren and Mum wrapped him in her arms and tried to soothe him while I stamped out the sparks on the hearthrug. When Cam stopped screaming long enough to breathe, Mum finally managed to calm him down.

With the poker I heaved the log up a bit to let the air get to the fire, which hadn't completely suffocated, but it had taken a shock and needed time to recover. Smoke

got into my eyes so I could hardly see, but I knew that the fire would burn up all right now that it was properly laid. Slowly, the smoke cleared. Ashes landed in our hair. Gray looked at me as if I'd pulled half a dozen rabbits out of a hat.

"Wow!" he said. "Where did you learn to do that?"

"At my grandparents' house," I muttered, but it didn't matter where I learned it, it mattered that Cam was wide-eyed and shaking in Mum's arms with his dog clamped to his chest. Gray took him at last, and presently Cam forgot to be terrified because he wanted to help Mum carry things into the kitchen. Gray simply brushed ashes from his sweater and went for another rummage through the cupboards where he found board games and jigsaws, so I left him to play. He tried to get Cam interested, but no way. Cam settled himself in front of the television with his dog in his arms, rocked from side to side, and glazed over.

At some point Mum suggested that I might like a hot bath and an early night and I hugged her, because she'd read my mind. That was exactly what I wanted. I ran a deep, steaming bath and slid down thankfully into the hot water.

I reckoned that with patience and ear mufflers I could just about cope with Cam, but Gray was infuriating, like a great big puppy, running from one thing to the next, wagging his tail – *Look at this, everyone! Look what I've found! Let's go for a walk, let's go to lots of places, let's set the house on fire!* A big, gangly, overgrown puppy! Perhaps in the morning I'd put on my wellies, go out in the snow, and throw sticks for Gray to fetch, but I'd had enough for one evening.

Still, I felt a lot better after my bath. I curled up in that sweet, cosy room with a book and a hot chocolate, looking up now and again to see the snow still falling past the window. I could cope with more of this. I don't know what time it was when I was drifting off to sleep, but I woke again with a jolt when doors slammed, and there was a lot of shouting, banging and crashing from the other bedroom. The floor shook gently. This, I found out, was Cam's bedtime routine, or the nearest he came to one. If I'd been that little black dog I would have hidden under a cushion and stayed there.

Even though I'd gone to bed early, I slept late. I was dressed and wandering about with a piece of toast in my hand when Cam yelled, "HORSES!"

Oh, help, he's up. I looked out and saw Peggy and Jayjay in their field with Cam hurtling towards them like the hound of hell. I'd seen what he could do to a snowman, so I wasn't going to wait and see what he did with the horses. I pulled on my boots and ran outside. At first I'd been worrying about Cam hurting the horses, poking them with a stick or something, then I realized that it might be the other way round. If he managed to get into the field he could get a donkey kick in the head – and in case you're wondering, there was no sign of Gray anywhere.

I stopped suddenly because Cam did. Without slowing down he stopped running and stood quite still, almost up to the tops of his wellies in the snow. He

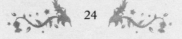

hadn't noticed me. Then he walked forward very slowly and calmly, lifting his welly-booted feet high out of the drifts and talking. I could hear every word.

"Hello, horse. Hello, donkey," he said gently. "Are you cold? Do you like snow? It's all right, I won't hurt you. Do you want something to eat?"

He was at the fence now, putting his hand up nervously to stroke Peggy's nose. She tossed her head and he snatched his hand back.

"Hello, donkey," he said, and Jayjay stood still, letting Cam stroke his nose. "You can't reach the nice grass, can you? I'll get some for you."

His hands were bare and pink with cold, but he bent and scraped about in the snow to pull up the grass. It was short and scrubby but he got a handful of it and held it out on his hand. When Jayjay nibbled at it he flinched. I wondered where the black dog was, then saw its little head poking out from under his coat.

"Hello, Cam," I said gently. He didn't look round – he was too fascinated with Jayjay, wanting to feed him and afraid of being bitten. "Look, shall I show you how to feed them? Would you like that?" I pulled up some grass and showed him how to offer it on a flat palm. "They won't bite. Their lips tickle, but you have to stand still."

He put grass on his palm and held his left wrist with his right hand to keep steady, so I put my hand under his. There was almost a little smile on his face but at the same time he was solemn, as if he was doing something very important.

"Shall we give them some apple?" I said, and at that he turned to me and really did smile, his deep, dark eyes brightening up. "You stay just where you are."

In the cottage Gray had spread a map on the table and was bending over it. From the sound of splashing water I knew Mum was in the shower.

"Don't worry about Cam," I called to Gray as I passed. "He's outside, he's fine."

"Oh, good," he said, then looked up and added, "Thanks." I pretended I hadn't heard and went back to Cam, who was gazing at Jayjay as if he'd fallen in love.

With my hand under his again we fed chunks of apple to Jayjay, and when Peggy pushed in I fed her and left Cam and Jayjay to look after each other. With his dark eyes bright and his gaze fixed on the donkey, the happiness glowed out of Cam. He pulled a face about getting donkey slaver on his hand, but I told him it was nothing to worry about and to rub it on his coat. Gray wasn't going to notice, was he?

I couldn't believe the change in Cam. Last night he'd beaten a snowman to death, then run round the house shooting things, sulked, and finally made an almighty racket going to bed. Now he was quiet and full of joy. Was it the horses that had made him so peaceful?

"I like animals," confided Cam happily, still watching Jayjay. "I like all of them. I want a dog but Daddy says we can't have one because we're out too much."

A thought struck me. "Who looks after you when your Daddy's working?" I asked. He shrugged, and avoided my eyes.

"I stay with Nicky," he said. "She's my childminder. Or sometimes Nan and Grandie come."

That was all. He was absorbed in feeding the animals and not interested in the adults in his life. When the horses had eaten every scrap of apple and some more tufts of grass, Gray called Cam in because he hadn't had breakfast yet.

Cam having breakfast was quite a performance. If there'd been anyone about I could have sold tickets. He didn't sit down, just walked round in circles eating a bowl of every kind of cereal with banana on top, while keeping his black dog jammed under his arm. I watched to see if he'd change direction and unwind himself, but I didn't like to suggest it in case he exploded.

To be fair, Gray stepped up to the mark after breakfast. We all went out in the bright cold morning with the snow squeaking under our boots, and built an enormous snowman. This time it stayed standing up. Then Mum chucked a snowball at Gray (go, Mum!) and all of us except Cam had a snowball fight. Cam said he didn't like snowball fights. Did he want to go inside and get warm? No, he didn't want to be alone in the house either, so he sat on the doorstep.

I couldn't just leave him there getting wet all the way through to his knickers. I took a densely packed snowball and knelt down beside him.

"Here, Cam," I said. "See if you can get Daddy." He shrank back. "Look," I whispered, "we'll hide round the corner of the house. Round here. Come and I'll show

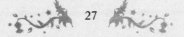

27

you. Then we'll jump out and throw the snowball and hide again."

He put his head down and wouldn't look at me.

"OK," I said. "I'll do it myself, then."

That worked. He wasn't going to let me have all the fun, so he jumped up and came with me. His first shot sailed past Gray but mine got him on the shoulder and I aimed the next one at Mum. Cam knocked it out of my hands with a glare that would have chilled me to the bone if I hadn't already been frozen.

"You don't throw snowballs at her," he told me sternly. *OK*. . . I threw one very gently at him instead, and rather to my surprise we had our own polite little snowball fight. We both stayed mostly dry because I aimed to miss and he couldn't hit a moving target, but he'd taken his gloves off and fingers were berry-red with cold. We were all going back indoors when Cam must have caught his foot on something under the snow, because he tripped and fell full length.

We all picked him up and I thought he'd make a fuss, but he was all right until he saw the thin red line of blood running down his wrist. You know how some children are funny about blood? Some adults, too. It was nothing, just a teeny cut, but he opened his little mouth and screamed so loudly it was painful.

"Put it in your mouth, Cam," I said, but he ignored me.

"Cam, it's all right," said Gray very calmly, and he put his hands firmly on Cam's shoulders. Cam shook him off, ran to Mum, and hurled himself into her arms.

"It's all right, Cam," she soothed. She stroked his hair and kissed the scratch. "Shh. We'll soon put that right." As she carried him indoors he clung like a scared little monkey, his fingers curled tightly into her sweater, his feet wrapped around her waist, his face crammed against her shoulder as if he'd die if he let go.

I stamped snow off my boots and turned to Gray. "Is he phobic about blood?" I asked, but I don't think he heard me. Then I saw the look on Gray's face.

Imagine that you've lost everything; you're a long way from home, no phone, no money, no anything. Then you see somebody coming, a paramedic or just somebody who looks kind and sensible and might, just might, help you – somebody who can make everything right. That's exactly how Gray looked, watching Mum as she soothed Cam and carried him indoors...

Don't look at her like that, I thought. *Please don't.*

Chapter Three

At lunch we talked about what we were going to do for the next few days. Gray had all those leaflets out again, (at least, the ones Mum hadn't taken away from him). Over the bread and soup he had a surprisingly sensible idea. He suggested that each of us choose one thing that we'd really love to do.

That didn't take long. Mum had fallen in love with the landscape, and all she wanted was a few hours to wander about with the camera. There was a wildlife park near us where they had little red squirrels, foxes, wildcats and all kinds of deer – even reindeer. It was called the Flora Kennedy Wildlife Park after a rich woman who got it started, but apparently everyone just called it "Flora's". Cam was dead keen to go there, and so was I. (I was hoping that the wildcats were well enclosed – those things are vicious. I'd read that they never attack without good reason, but you don't go up to one and ask what it calls a good reason.)

They asked me to choose a day out, and I was still thinking. The thing I most wanted was to go to Flora's, and we'd already planned that trip. The only other thing I wanted was time to be left alone with a couple of books and my stash of lemon bonbons.

"I just want time by myself to read," I said. (I didn't mention the lemon bonbons.) Mum and Gray asked me if I was sure that was all I wanted, and I managed to convince them that I really didn't want to climb a mountain and, truly and honestly, I hadn't set my heart on the tartan museum. Or the pottery. Just leave me alone with a book!

Action Man wanted to go skiing. That was fine. He could ski all he liked, so long as I didn't have to join in. Sledging down snowy hills is fun, but just in case you've forgotten what I think about the other thing, here is:

THE LIBBY SUTTON VERY SENSIBLE GUIDE TO SKIING, or JUST DON'T DO IT

"To ski" – the act of hurtling down an icy mountain much too fast, with pointy sticks.

Skiing was invented by people living up mountains in Norway or Switzerland or somewhere else where if they didn't learn to ski, they'd be stuck in a hut from November

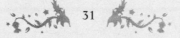

to March with no company except goats and a cuckoo clock and they'd go totally round the silly tree. If they needed to buy anything or see the doctor or take soup to the ancient granny on the other side of the mountain, skiing was the only way to do it.

Some people ski for fun. Yes, they really do. Blessed St Father Christmas, have mercy.

Mum said she'd go straight out after lunch with the camera, and the afternoon would be her day out. The wildlife place didn't open on Sundays and Mondays in winter, so the ski trip would be Monday, we'd have the whole day at Flora's on Tuesday, then travel home on Wednesday. Cam got grumpy about having to wait until Tuesday for his treat, so he banged the table, pushed out his lower lip till it looked like a cocktail sausage, took a running kick at the wall, stamped off to his bedroom and banged the door. Perhaps on Tuesday, if he was Sweet Funny Little Cam, I'd walk round with him, show him the animals, and tell him all about them. If he was Cam the Unspeakable I'd shove him in the nearest empty enclosure with a label on the door: WILD HIGHLAND GOBLIN. DO NOT STICK YOUR FINGER THROUGH THE BARS.

He went into super-sulk when Mum went out with her camera, because he didn't want her to go. He stood at the window with his dog under his arm and his pet

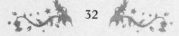

lip sticking out like a shelf, watching until she was out of sight, then stomped off to his bedroom. Gray did make an effort to get him to go out and play in the snow, but no, Cam wasn't having it. That was Gray's problem, not mine.

I built up the fire to a good crackling blaze, turned an armchair towards it, and snuggled in with my book. Now and again I looked up at the snow to see the sparkle of it, and the soft blue shadows. A few fresh flakes fell. Once again it was magical, more magical than you could expect anything to be on earth. A little way off I could see the edge of the forest, and with the snow on the fir trees you could expect to find a gingerbread house in there. I wriggled further back into the chair, snug and smug and very contented.

I'd been there for about an hour when Cam wandered in with his dog under his arm. He stood at the window watching the falling snow and singing the same song *over and over again. Flat.* I suspected he might be doing it on purpose and pretended not to notice, but I could only stand it for so long. I tried to concentrate, but I was distracted by thoughts of Cam, thoughts to do with scruff of neck and toe of boot, you know the sort of thing. Finally I went to my room. It was colder in there, but I had a duvet and I wouldn't be able to hear him.

Presently, I noticed something bobbing past the window. About two minutes later it happened again. I kept watching. Cam was marching round and round the house, planting his feet down hard with a look of

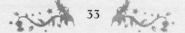

great concentration on his face. A few minutes later he came back the other way. It made me laugh and I waved to him, which was probably a mistake because his little face lit up, and a minute later he came running straight into my room.

"You should knock before you come in here," I said, keeping my eyes on my book. Cam ran outside, knocked, and came straight back in.

"When you've knocked, you have to wait until I tell you to come in," I said.

He ran outside, knocked, and waited. What could I do?

"OK, Cam," I said. I took one last look at the rest of the paragraph, put in a marker, and closed the book. "What do you want to tell me?"

"You haven't told me to come in," he said.

"Come in, Cam."

He walked in like a little pageboy. "I've been making tracks!" he said. "I looked for tracks and there weren't any, just birds, so I made some tracks and tracked them, but I knew where they were. Please will you come and make some tracks for me to follow?"

He'd asked politely. I looked out of the window and checked my watch. We'd have a couple of hours before the light started to fade, and he was on "Good Little Cam" setting. But if Cam thought that I was going to tramp about so he could tramp about after me...

"Tell you what," I said, "shall we go out together for a long walk and see if we can find any animal tracks? If it's all right with Daddy?"

He charged off to tell Gray, but a good lunch and a warm fire had sent Action Man to sleep, so Cam had to wake him up first. This involved a lot of shouting so I hid in the kitchen. Gray had fallen asleep by the fire and was just very glad that he wasn't expected to go with us. While Cam got his boots back on I went to the kitchen to collect a couple of apples, and had what I have to say was the most brilliant idea. There was a tea tray beside the cooker – a big old-fashioned wooden one with a rim round it and handles. I knew we had some rope in the back of our car, and fortunately Mum hadn't locked it. By the time Cam was ready, so was I.

"What's that thing?" he said.

Well thanks, you little horror. You're supposed to be delighted.

"It's a sledge!" said Gray. *Well done, that man.*

"It looks like a tray," said Cam stubbornly.

"Please yourself," I said. "If you don't want to ride on it, I will, and you can pull me along."

That settled it. I pulled him along on the tea-tray sledge and we both looked for tracks, but as Cam said, there were only bird prints.

"We have to go up that hill!" he yelled, pointing ahead. It wasn't so much a hill, just gently rising ground. Even so I wasn't pulling the sledge all the way up there, and I told him so.

"I can climb it!" he shouted, and off he went! He was so padded out with winter layers that he looked like a little brown bear clambering up the hill, and I picked up the tray to follow him. At the top he plodded

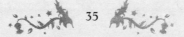

along with his head down.

"Only birds," he said when I caught up, but I was wondering what sort of bird had such big pronounced claws. Then I looked up, and caught sight of something. If it hadn't moved, I swear I wouldn't have seen it. It was quite round, and beautifully white.

"Cam!" I whispered. I knelt beside him, putting a finger to my lips and pointing with the other hand. "You see those trees? Just down a bit, and left – that's this way. Keep watching."

"I can't see anything," he whispered back.

"Keep watching. You'll see it when it moves." Then I realized that I hadn't told him what "it" was. "It's a ptarmigan!"

Ptarmigan (with a silent "t") are a kind of grouse, and their winter feathers blend with the landscape. This one was as plump and round as a Christmas pudding, and I was willing it to move so that Cam could see it. Then it turned its head, and there was a flash of deep red from the patch above its eye. Cam gasped, and flinched back.

"You don't see them in many places," I said, "just up here in the Highlands."

"Why has it got blood on it?" he asked.

"That's not blood," I said, but I could see why he thought so. "It has a red mark near its eye. They all have that."

He relaxed after that, and we watched it pick its way across the drifts like a self-important little poodle. Cam's eyes shone. I thought he'd forgotten to breathe. When

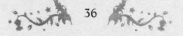

it flew away he gave a sad little sigh, ran at the nearest drift, kicked snow into my face, and laughed loudly.

"Don't, Cam," I said firmly.

"Sorry," said Cam, which astonished me so much that I didn't know what to say. I glanced round for inspiration and saw a good slope for sledging down, so that's what we did. Yes, *we*! We took turns and, what a surprise, Cam *liked* taking turns. He enjoyed the routine, the process of climbing up the hill with the empty sledge and passing it to me. If I hadn't moved things on he'd still be there now, but I got bored before he did. I checked my phone now and again just to see if there was any signal, but of course there wasn't. Not in a place like that.

"What do you think we might find over there, Cam?" I asked, pointing to the Christmas tree forest. Sun glinted from the branches and a bird flew from a treetop. It looked full of secrets.

"Will there be any termy . . . termigers in there?" he asked.

"Ptarmigan? I don't know," I said. "We can have a look."

"On the sledge," he said, settling down on it. Oh, it was the *sledge* now, not the tea tray! It occurred to me that Ailsa might not be pleased at her tea tray being dragged through the snow but it was a bit late for that. With any luck she wouldn't find out.

The forest had an air of secrecy about it, and after the glare of sunshine on snow it was so shady that at first I couldn't see a thing. There wasn't so much snow

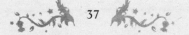

37

under the trees, so Cam had to get up and walk while I carried the tray. Pine cones and needles lay under our feet, and Cam picked up a cone.

"It's gone rotten," he said.

It looked ragged, there wasn't much left but the core. I put my hand out for it and saw his fingers tighten as he glared at me.

"May I see, please?" I said. "I won't take it away."

He gave me his "I hate you" scowl, but he handed it over. I held it up to the light and turned it.

"It's not rotten," I said. "It's been a squirrel's dinner. Can you see?"

I put it back into his hands and showed him how it had been stripped to the core by sharp little teeth. Cam gazed into the treetops with his eyes and mouth wide open.

"Are there squirrels in here?" he asked.

"There must be," I said. "This is just the sort of place they like. But they're hiding."

At this point, you need:

THE LIBBY SUTTON ABSOLUTELY TRUE AND ACCURATE GUIDE TO RED SQUIRRELS

(NB The grey ones are just rats with bushy tails.)

Red squirrels are so sorted. They don't hibernate. They store food and have a quiet December with their paws up drinking hazelnut hot choccie and watching Christmas TV like those rabbits I was telling you about. They snooze a lot. How sensible is that? Then in January it's the first mating season of the year. While most wild animals are either snoring in their nests or hunting for food, red squirrels are out in their very best winter coats chasing each other through the treetops. In the spring, there are lots of baby squirrels.

"If you're very quiet, you might see one," I whispered, so Cam walked along gazing up into the trees. When a flash of red fur ran across the path in front of him he nearly fell over it.

"Look!" I grabbed his arm and pointed. "Squirrel! It went that way. Keep watching."

Cam was all eyes – huge eyes! The squirrel shinned up a tree, its long tail trailing behind it, then leapt on to a branch. Oh yes! Another one jumped out at it, and the two of them ran in circles round the tree, leaping like acrobats, twirling their tails round branches, their eyes bright and their ears sharp and alert. They sprang to the next tree, then the next, and at last we lost sight of them.

"You're so lucky!" I whispered. "Most people never see one!"

"And there's a cat!" he said. "A great big cat, look!"

My stomach had tightened before I even looked. I hoped he was wrong. He wasn't.

A few metres away into the forest was a fallen tree.

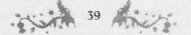

Crouched on the trunk was a big, solid-framed wildcat with a striped coat as thick and deep as a snowdrift. Its tail, hanging down beside it, twitched from side to side – a stripy brush of a tail – and its big, sharp ears were flattened back. Wild, glaring green eyes were fixed on us and they terrified me. My legs felt weak.

I'd only ever seen wildcats in pictures before, but believe me, when you see one you know you've seen it. Wildcats are savage, and this one was poised, its paws curled under its shoulders, ready to spring.

Enchanted forests are dangerous places. The cat was in its own territory. We were intruders.

But, remembering what I knew about wildcats, I could tell that this was all wrong. Wildcats don't hang around waiting to be noticed. They avoid people. They hunt at night. This one was wide awake, alert, and watching us.

They'd rather warn you off than fight, I knew that. They only attack if they feel threatened. I took Cam's hand and backed away slowly, not wanting to hurry in case we scared it.

"We have to go now," I whispered. "The cat doesn't want us here. Be very quiet. Look down! Don't look her in the eyes."

We backed steadily away, not too fast, not too slow, and I held the tray in front of Cam as a shield. *They don't attack if they don't need to,* I told myself. *It'll be fine.* Then it crouched lower, a terrible snarl came from its throat, and its claws curled.

"Cam, run!" I ordered. "Fast as you can!"

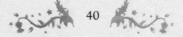

Either I used the right voice or he recognized the danger, because he was off like a shot. If we were separated the cat couldn't go for us both at once, and I was nearer.

The cat was hunched up, settling its hind legs, ready to spring. With the tray in front of my face, I slipped an apple out of my pocket.

The cat leapt. I hurled the apple at it hard, kicked up snow, and ran for my life, expecting with every breath to feel claws in the back of my neck. When I caught up with Cam I grabbed his hand and nearly dragged him out of the forest, not stopping until we were clear of the trees and I knew the cat hadn't followed. We were both out of breath. The snow was twinkling at us, the light was almost too strong and too clear, and we could see the cottage.

Cam didn't know how much danger we'd been in, but I was shaking. I could feel my heart thumping like an engine. The cottage was ahead of us and the forest lay behind like a scene from a fairy tale again – a dark fairy tale. I took a deep breath to pull myself together, and knelt down in front of Cam. His dark eyes were brimful of tears.

"It's all right now," I said. "Well done. You did everything right."

His face gathered into a scowl. With both hands he hit me so hard that I fell backwards in the snow. "I hate you!" he screamed. "You're bad!"

He aimed a kick at me, but I rolled over and got up as he went on pounding me with both fists. He picked

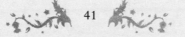

up snow and threw it in my face. I grabbed at him and held him with one hand round his arms and the other round his legs, not tightly enough to hurt him but firmly enough to stop him doing me any more damage.

"You're bad! Let me go!" He screamed as if he was calling on every crow and every hare in the forest to help him. "You're bad and horrible and I *hate* you! I *hate* you! I'll tell my dad about you! I'll tell your mum! Let me go!"

He hit a pitch that could have shattered glass, screamed and screamed again. I didn't know much about kids, but I could see that the only thing to do was to kneel in the freezing snow holding on to him until he'd stormed himself out. I admit I wished he'd get on with it. I was wearing waterproofs but they didn't keep out the cold.

"You're hurting me," he said sullenly, but I knew I wasn't. He added "ouch" so unconvincingly that I wanted to laugh, then he pretended to sob, and the pretend sobbing turned into real sobbing until he softened in my arms and I sat him on my lap and rocked him. At last, when all the fight had raged out of him, he looked up at me. His eyes were red and puffy and his face blotchy with crying.

"You shouldn't throw things at animals," he said. "It's cruel. You threw an apple. You kicked snow at it, you might have hurt it. You told me not to kick snow at you. I'm going to kick snow right in your face." He gave me a look of reproach that made me feel properly told off. "I didn't think you would do things like that."

I hadn't meant him to see that. The little brat must have looked round.

"Cam, sweetheart, I don't usually do things like that," I insisted. "I've never thrown anything at an animal before, or kicked snow, or anything like that. But that wasn't a nice kitty, it was a wildcat, and that means it's a fierce animal that might have hurt you. Like a. . ." – I thought of big cats – "like a jaguar or a tiger. Big hunting cats. Did you see those claws? Did you see its teeth, Cam? I didn't want to hurt it; I just had to distract it so that you could get away. And you did get away; you're safe, and that's what matters. All right?"

"Are you sorry?" he demanded.

"I'm sorry that you're upset," I said. I wasn't going to apologize for saving him from a wild animal with psychopathic tendencies. "The cat will be fine; she's fast and clever and she knows how to look after herself. She's probably laughing at us."

She's more likely to be tearing sparrows apart, I thought, but Cam seemed soothed. He sniffed and I gave him a tissue. Looking up, I saw that the sun was lower and there were reflections of gold across the snow.

"It's going to be a beautiful sunset," I said. "I think it's time we got back, don't you? We've had an exciting day. Do you like hot chocolate?"

Hot chocolate was definitely the right thing to suggest. He was so keen to get back to the cottage that he forgot about the sledge and ran on ahead. Outside, we stopped to talk to Peggy and Jayjay, and we were still there when Ailsa arrived in her sheepskin coat and boots.

"I see you've made a sledge," she said with approval. "What a good idea! My sisters and I used to go sledging on tea trays."

"I'll clean it," I promised.

"Och, it's only snow," she said. I really liked Ailsa.

We helped her put Peggy and Jayjay in their stable for the night, with Cam holding Jayjay's lead rope and me hovering beside him to grab it – or grab him – if necessary.

"You're a natural," said Ailsa. "You know just the way to handle him." I didn't know if she meant Cam or the donkey.

Chapter Four

All of us except Gray had been tramping about in the snow all day and the only things we could think of were hot drinks, hot food and the fire. It turned out that Gray, give him his due, liked to cook. Cam might not get enough of his father's attention, but he wouldn't starve. Gray made a mean risotto with flavours in it that I'd never tasted before, but it was just wonderful and moreish, a perfect winter evening meal, and he made heaps of it. We sat down round the table together, the fire flickered in the grate, and it was good.

It would have been even better if Cam could have sat still for five minutes but he was dotting about like a ping-pong ball, getting up to look out and see if it was snowing, running to the kitchen for ketchup or butter or a drink or whatever else he'd decided he wanted, playing with his food and generally being so annoying that I suspected he was doing it on purpose. Even while he did that he talked non-stop about what we'd been doing, every snowball and every ride down the hill. He must have been counting!

"It was my turn, then it was Libby's turn, then it was my turn. . ." When Gray said "not with your mouth full, Cam", Cam would close his mouth, gather himself together, gulp it all down and then go on talking. He must have had the stomach of a goat. Forcing down a mouthful of risotto ruined with tomato ketchup he said:

"We found a wildcat – a great big one!"

"A wildcat?" repeated Gray. "What, really wild?" *Bless!* He went on, "I didn't know there were any of those left. Do you mean a *feral* cat?"

"No, it was a really wild wildcat. Libby said it was," insisted Cam, and looked at me to back him up.

Up to now I'd kept quiet about that encounter. I mean, I hadn't actually *taken* Cam to see a staring vampire-toothed madcat, but it might not sound like that.

"Yes it was," I said calmly, as if it was no big deal. "It was amazing, we were very lucky to see it. They're extremely rare."

"It wanted to jump on me!" explained Cam proudly. Gray opened his mouth and nothing came out.

"It's fine," I said. "It didn't get near us." (OK, so it depended on what you meant by "near".)

"All the same, aren't those things dangerous?" said Gray, looking at me in a stern, teachery sort of way. He

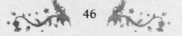

had no business to do that! It's not as if I'd known the wildcat was there! I knew what I was talking about, and he hadn't a clue.

"They're only dangerous if you provoke them, and we didn't," I said. "They avoid people. It'll stay in the trees where it can find food and shelter."

I braced myself for the next bit because I was sure Cam was about to tell them about naughty Libby throwing things at the cat. But all he said was, "Libby made it go away," then he stuffed his mouth with risotto and said:

"I putcha zhonkey do bedge." He swallowed, and repeated, "I put the donkey to bed. He likes me. Ailsa said he did. Ailsa said she used to go sledging. Mum used to take me on the sledge, didn't she? Didn't she, Dad? Have you got the photographs?"

After dinner Gray put up some pictures on his laptop: images of a smiling woman pulling a sledge down a snowy street. Cam hadn't changed much; he was just younger with a rounder, more babyish face beaming out from a cocoon of snowsuit, hat with ears, Gruffalo scarf, mitts and wellies. Pulling the sledge was a simply beautiful young woman with deep, dark eyes like Cam's and wild black curls escaping from under a woolly hat. Her cheeks were pink with cold, she was striding forwards, and she seemed to be laughing at the camera. She looked so alive!

"I'd forgotten that one was on there," said Gray quietly.

"That's my mummy!" said Cam proudly.

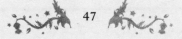

47

"She's beautiful," I said. I know it should have been "she *was* beautiful", but that didn't seem right.

"Yes, she's very beautiful," said Cam. "Dad's got that picture in his study. In my bedroom I've got one from when I was a baby and one on the beach when I was little…"

He took over the laptop and began to chant his unstoppable way through the pictures. I saw Mum put a hand on Gray's arm, and Gray just said that it was all right, and it was best to let Cam go on. "That's me and my mum on the slide, that's me and my mum with hats on because she'd been to hospital and her hair fell out, so we all wore hats…" All the time I wondered what this was doing to Gray, all of this "my mum this, my mum that, my mum when she was poorly".

Gray watched the images as Cam flicked them across the screen and there was a soft, sad smile on his face. Gray watched the pictures, and Mum watched Gray.

"Cam, show Libby your favourite one," Gray said.

Gleefully, Cam whizzed through until he found the picture he wanted. It showed that small, babyish Cam with his mummy again, but this time they were holding two kittens that were mostly white with black patches and the most adorable little faces.

"I like that because it's me and Mum *and* animals," he said. "That's Auntie Liz's cats when they were little."

"That's enough time in front of a screen," said Gray suddenly. (I don't think he minded really; I think Gray couldn't bear to see any more pictures of his wife.) "It's time you had a bath."

In the last half hour I'd begun to feel sorry for Gray and think that he wasn't such a rubbish parent after all. But now he was snatching Cam from an activity he was enjoying and telling him to go for a bath. Did he think that was going to happen without a fight? It seemed as if every time I saw a good side of Gray he went back to "clever but clueless" again, and Mum really didn't need another of those.

"I'm not having a bath," announced Cam. His mouth set in that hard scowl and he glowered at his father. I had to fight so, so hard not to laugh.

"That's OK," I said. "It means I can have all the bubbles."

Cam bounced up as if he was on springs. "BUBBLES!" (The shout was so loud, I winced.) "Have we got bubbles?"

"Libby can do magic," said Mum. "I'm sure she can magic up some bubbles."

Cam was off like a rocket to get his pyjamas, and while he did that I ran the water and put in a good squeeze of washing-up liquid. When he was bathed and warm and tucked in bed, he wanted Mum to tell him a story, so I left them to it. I remembered the way he'd looked in the afternoon, raging and storming at me because of the wildcat, almost like a wildcat himself, lost and fierce and ready to fight. Now he was glazed and contented, snuggled up against Mum.

At that point, I knew I'd done my bit. A thank you from Gray for looking after his son all afternoon would have been nice, but I wasn't holding my breath for one.

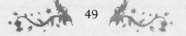

I wanted one more walk outside in the snow in the darkness, just as far as the pony field so that I could stand under the night sky in the snow, then spend the evening with a book. But as I left I saw the look on Gray's face as he watched Mum and Cam snuggling up with a storybook, and it was like seeing a little boy looking at his dream Christmas present in a shop window. Poor Gray. I knew he didn't always do the right thing, but all the same – poor Gray.

Don't set your hearts on this too much, I thought. *Any of you. It could all go horribly wrong.*

So there I was, thinking that Gray might just be a halfway reasonable person. The next day was ski day.

I was woken by a lot of clumping about and banging of car doors because Gray was already getting organized, striding out to the car with all this ski stuff. (By "the car" I mean his car, which was bigger and posher than ours and better at getting through snow, or so Gray kept telling us.) By the time Peggy and Jayjay were out, Gray was so keen to get away that he was practically hopping from one foot to the other like a little kid, and he *wouldn't stop talking*. He'd have to wait, though, because Mum was helping Cam with his coat and wellies. It had to be Mum; Cam wouldn't let anyone else help him.

I didn't begrudge Gray his ski day. I just wished we didn't all have to go with him. But he'd persuaded Mum that she wanted to go, so that meant we all had to go – and we simply had to try skiing, didn't we, because it

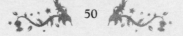

was *such fun!* I knew it would be *such fun* because he wouldn't stop telling me:

"It's scary at first, but once you're underway it's just the most amazing..." "There is nothing in the world like it..." "Just try it, if you just try..." "If you want to have a go on a dry ski slope I'm sure there's one near where you live where you can practise..."

"I know, but I'd rather not," I said, because I couldn't say, "yes, Gray, I know you love jumping off mountains, but you're a dangerous idiot who should be locked up for his own safety and everybody else's." *Would he ever shut up?*

"If you just try it once..." (*No, he wouldn't.*) "If you just try the skis on..."

I gave up arguing and looked past him at the white-laced trees, the rough bobbled branches and the far off silvery waterfalls. The whiteness was getting tiring. Gray could say all he liked, I would just refuse to have those skis put on my feet. He didn't know what he was up against.

"And if he sees you skiing, Cam might have a go," said Gray.

"That's up to him," I snapped. "It's nothing to do with me." There was an unpleasant silence.

I turned my back, walked over to Peggy and Jayjay, and stayed with them, smoothing their necks and talking to them until I'd got Gray out of my system. It seemed such a mean thing to do to put pressure on me like that, wanting me to try skiing to encourage Cam. Excuse me? Who's responsible for Cam?

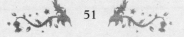

51

Without turning round, I knew Gray was coming toward me. I'd made it perfectly clear that the conversation was over.

"I'm sorry if I upset you, Libby," he said. "I didn't mean to."

I shrugged, not turning round. "'S'all right," I said. It wasn't, but that was the easiest thing to say. The whole scene made me feel awkward. It usually is when someone apologizes to you. It went quiet after that.

Sitting in the car I wished I'd brought sunglasses, the sun was so bright. I sort of understood that if you were into skiing it was a perfect day for it, with those rough white crags inviting you to the challenge. Soon we could see the ski lifts running on their pulleys up the hillside like tramlines in the sky, carrying the skiers in their bright colourful ski suits and hats. There was one of those big grey-and-glass reception buildings for information, loos and this-is-where-you-pay-for-stuff, and on the far side of it...

Cam sprang into the air: one huge jump, vertical take-off and landing. Then he ran round us all in a circle and grabbed Gray's hand.

"TRAIN!" he bellowed. (I'll swear a golden eagle dropped out of the sky in shock.) He was right about the train, though. On the other side of the reception block was a small platform with an old-fashioned steam train blowing puffy clouds at the cold, clear sky, like something from a storybook. Cam's eyes shone.

"It's a funicular railway," said Gray. "That means it can go up and down steep hills."

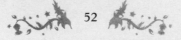

"I'll take him on the train if you like," I offered quickly. I'd slipped back into the role of nanny, but it meant that I'd be well out of the way of the slopes. Gray looked undecided. He hadn't managed to get me on skis, and he was desperate to persuade Cam – but Cam had shut his mouth in that determined little line and I was learning that it wasn't easy to make him do something he didn't want to. I still had bruises from the day before.

"Does it just go up and down the mountain all day?" asked Gray.

I went to reception to see what I could find out. At the top of the mountain was a visitor centre called the Eyrie that had only opened that winter. It had exhibitions, viewing galleries and a cafe. *Cafe!* Talk about a no-brainer! I reported back.

"It's fine, Gray," I said. "You and Mum do all the skiing you like, Cam and I can go on the train to the Eyrie."

What a nice, sensible girl Libby is. How thoughtful! How capable. If Gray wasn't thinking this, he should have been. Anyway, Gray and Mum handed over some cash and went off to sort out their landing-on-your-bum-in-the-snow day and Cam and I took the train.

He was so excited about that train, he started going into hyper mode. All the time I was buying the tickets he jumped up and down, looking at that train like a cat at a bird box. As soon as we were through the barrier he shot off like a rocket, and he would have barged straight past a woman with one child by the hand and another in a buggy if I hadn't grabbed him.

"Cam, we don't push in," I told him. He wriggled furiously, but I held on. Even after he stopped wriggling I could feel the tension in his arm, the resentment at anything that came between him and that train. The day before nothing had happened that I couldn't cope with, even the wildcat, but this time I could barely keep the lid on him. Once we were on the train he bounced up and down so hard I thought he'd fall right through the seat. A woman gave him a bit of a look and I blanked her. *OK,* I thought, *OK, he's a brat. But he's my little br—*

Little brat. That's what I mean. My little brat. Not little bro. . . I nearly thought "brother" but only because I was stressed and some ignorant stranger was looking down her nose at us.

"Cam, keep a sharp lookout," I said. "We might see deer. Or a white hare."

"We might see termygots."

"Ptarmigan."

"Will there be wildcats?"

"No," I said. I hoped not, at least. I'd had enough of those for one holiday. Then the train made a noise like a cross cow and off we went, Cam staring out of the window, all eyes, holding his black dog up against the glass so it could see. When we got off at the other end I knew we'd made a good call.

The Eyrie was the most fantastic place. It was roomy, bright and modern, with displays and a proper, gleaming, clean cafe, and yet it was right on top of the wildest place I'd ever been. I'll try to describe it to you,

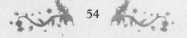

but I don't know if I can make you feel what it was like to be there. It was like being in a glass palace in the sky, and it was circular – you could walk all round it and see amazing views of sky, mountain and waterfalls, all different. Nearly all the walls were windows, and there was a balcony, too. It was worth being out there, even though the cold made me gasp, because I really did feel I was walking in the mountains – but I didn't want to stay there long in case Cam tried to throw himself off.

Cam dragged me off to see an exhibition of "The Secret Life of the Mountain", showing you all the things you might see up there if you're lucky (including termygots). Granny and Grandpa would have loved it, and I wished they could see it. Along the windows there were binoculars chained to a shelf so you couldn't run off with them, and Cam tried every single pair while I sat on a bench and soaked up the view. It was so vast, so magnificent, with blue shadows on crags, sparkling snow to the south and the liquid silver of streams. . .

"Cam, look!" A white hare sat up, shook its ears, and sprinted across the snow. Cam wasn't listening; he was gazing into the binoculars, and his shout of "DEER!" could have shattered the windows. I was afraid we'd get kicked out, but we didn't. I looked where he was pointing and there they were, far away: red deer grazing on a hill. Cam could see them perfectly and he was alight with happiness, staring down the binoculars with a big smile on his face – then he rushed headlong at me just the way he'd run at the snowman, flung his arms round me, and hugged the breath out of me. What was that for? Was he just so happy that he needed to hug someone? I hugged him back, hard. How could I not?

There were activity tables with things for children to do – jigsaws, colouring, that sort of thing. Cam drifted over to one and we sat by the window with an apple juice for him and a hot chocolate for me, while I helped him with the puzzles and watched little flurries of snow dance past the window as if they were playing a game. I was thinking what an amazing place this would be after dark when the stars were out and, by the way, what were we doing about lunch, when Mum and Gray arrived all bright-eyed and pink from the cold like kids who've just come in from a snowball fight.

"That was so exciting!" said Mum, and then she was telling me all about it and laughing, fizzing with excitement and happiness, and Gray was saying how well she'd done. At a table near the window we ate toasties, and anybody looking at us would have thought we were a real family – though they might have wondered where Cam got those huge dark eyes from with the look that still puzzled me. We looked like a family, but we weren't, and we might never be – but Gray hadn't said or done anything really stupid since he walked into the Eyrie, so we were happy enough. At first I was on edge in case Cam suddenly got shouty or kicked someone, but he behaved himself, and eventually I relaxed.

When we'd finished eating Cam hauled them off on a tour of the Eyrie and I was thinking that we'd probably go back to the cottage soon when Gray turned to Mum and said, "What do you think, Kate? Back to the slopes? Libby, that's if you and Cam are OK up here?"

I almost said "certainly not", just to see the look on his face. He could have asked me first, right? But I didn't mind. Cam was setting up the Jenga on one of the tables, I had a book, and Mum looked keen to go back to the ski slopes, so why not?

"No problem," I said. "I'll see you back up here when you're finished."

Off went Mum and Gray like a pair of happy hikers in a story. Cam played Jenga against himself, I took out my book, and now and again we'd stop what we were doing and just look out of the windows. Something that might have been an eagle circled the mountain tops.

Cam tired of Jenga and worked his way round the tables doing all the jigsaws. I began to read more slowly, because I only had one book with me and I didn't want to finish it too soon. Cam grew bored. I read him a story but he soon lost interest. The thing that might have been an eagle packed up its wings and went home. I looked at my watch. It was time Gray stopped playing penguins and got back to us.

Chapter Five

Cam said he was hungry, so I bought flapjacks and more drinks. Other visitors arrived, looked round, had a coffee and went away again. The people who worked at the cafe kept looking at us; they must have thought we'd moved in. I began to wonder what time they closed. I tried to call Mum to ask her when they expected to be back, but the cafe guy – a rather cute ginger with nice eyes – said there was no signal up there because it was too high.

"Can we go on the train again?" asked Cam too loudly.

"We'll have to, to get back down," I said.

"Can we go on the train again?"

"Yes, Cam, when your daddy and my mum get back."

I checked my watch. I'd have to ask the cafe guys when the last train left.

"Can we go on the train again?"

"Yes, Cam, I told you, when Daddy and Kate get here."

At first I was annoyed with Gray and Mum, and then I got worried. I just wanted them to walk through the door. The sky, and the shadows on the snow, grew darker, and if Cam asked me once more about that train...

"Excuse me, is your name Libby Sutton?"

I'd been gazing out of the window without really seeing anything when I heard somebody say my name. It was the cute ginger and he held out the phone, the one from the landline.

It was probably nothing. That's what I told myself as I took the phone – *it's probably nothing.* But the thought at the front of my head was that somebody must have been hurt, and I couldn't bear it to be Mum.

"Libby, it's Gray," said the voice at the other end. "Don't worry, it's all right – but your mum took a bit of a tumble."

You idiot, I thought. Whatever had happened, it had to be Gray's fault. I sat down. *You stupid, selfish, useless idiot.*

"What sort of a tumble?" I asked.

"She's OK – she's conscious, she's talking," he said. "But her leg is hurt and she can't stand up. The first-aiders are here, and they've sent for an ambulance."

"Then she's not OK," I said. She couldn't stand up, what was OK about that? "I'm on my way. Where are you?"

"Take the next train down," he said. "At the bottom, tell them who you are and somebody will bring you to the piste." Then he added, "Bring Cam."

Bring Cam. Thank you, Gray – if you hadn't told me to bring him I would have left him up a mountain. There was no problem getting Cam to go; he was looking forward to the train, his daddy, and the possibility of seeing more animals. His coat was on before you could say "termygotties".

"My mum's hurt her leg a bit," I explained as we waited for the train. "We have to see if she's all right."

I'd made it as low-key as possible, but the questions started. What had happened? Where was she? Where was Daddy? Was Daddy all right? *Yes*, I said, *Daddy's all right*, but to be honest I couldn't have cared less. All the way down Cam asked questions, rattling from one to the next without waiting for answers. This time he wasn't interested in the window. He was jittery and anxious, fidgeting, wriggling and turning the dog over and over in his hands, and all the time I told myself it would be fine. Or it probably would. Mum was a bit hurt. People do get hurt skiing, it happens all the time. She'd be fine.

She'll be fine, I had to keep telling myself. *She'll be fine. She isn't screaming in pain, she isn't going to spend the rest of her life in a wheelchair. It's her leg, not her head. She isn't...* But all the time, somewhere else in my head I was storming with rage at Gray, grabbing him by his coat, shaking him and shouting in his face: *You had to make her go skiing! You'd had a great morning,*

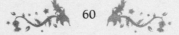

60

*but that wasn't enough; you had to drag her out there
again this afternoon and you couldn't even look after her!
What were you doing, whizzing down the piste, showing
off, while my mum struggled to keep up with you and got
hurt?*

The train jolted to a stop. At the station a woman in
a high-visibility jacket was waiting for us with a kind
of snow buggy like a larger version of a kids' pedal car,
ready to whizz us off to Mum.

"In you go, Cam," I said.

"No!" he shouted, wrenching his hand out of mine.
"We have to find Kate!"

"This lady's taking us to Kate," I said. Did I have to
explain everything? "In you get."

From the throng of hi-vis jackets I could tell where
Mum was long before I saw her. Gray was there,
standing with a ski in one hand as if it was the guilty ski
and he'd just arrested it. When he saw us getting out
of the buggy he came to meet us, and Cam would have
made a dash for him if I hadn't held on tight. I didn't
want another injury, and besides, I couldn't risk him
hurling himself at Mum if she was hurt.

"It's OK, Libby, she'll be all right," said Gray. "Her
ski sort of swerved and she lost her balance and fell
badly. There's an ambulance coming."

"Stay with Daddy now, Cam," I said, not even
looking at Gray. He could take responsibility for his
own son for a change. Then I pushed through the
crowd to Mum, knelt in the snow beside her, and took
her gloved hand in both of mine.

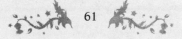

Poor Mum was still lying in the snow but they'd got her on to a stretcher with a pillow under her head, and wrapped her in blankets. She was shaking, and I suspected it was shock rather than cold. Her face was grey-white, and even though she smiled bravely up at me I could see pain in her eyes. Something inside me twisted. I hoped she couldn't tell how scared I was, seeing her like that. I had to be strong.

"I've done something really stupid and hurt my leg," she said, but her voice was weak. "I'm so sorry, sweetheart."

"Don't be silly!" I said, with what I hoped was a comforting smile. "It wasn't your fault! You just keep still and we'll get you better." There was a shuffling in the crowd and I knew that Gray was behind me. Couldn't he see that this was just about Mum and me? I hoped he wasn't letting Cam see Mum like this. I glanced over my shoulder and saw Cam clinging on to Gray and pressing his face against his dad's legs.

"The ambulance is at reception, Kate," said Gray. "We'll soon have you in hospital."

And you can stop pretending that you've got it all under control. It's the paramedics who are helping her, not you. When the crew loaded her into the ambulance I said that I wanted to go with her.

"You can follow in the car with your dad," suggested the ambulance woman.

"He's not my dad," I said, loudly enough for Gray to hear me.

*

As soon as we got to the hospital Cam yelled, "I hate hospitals!" and found a wall to kick. Gray took no notice; he was talking to receptionists and nurses while sticking to Mum like a Siamese twin, and as far as he was concerned, he was The Grown-Up In Charge and I was The Big Child Who Looks After The Little Child. (The Little Child curled up in a corner, so I left him to get on with it.)

When Mum was wheeled away on a trolley, Gray said, "Libby, look after Cam. I'll stay with Kate."

I looked into his eyes, not smiling. "He's your son," I said. "And she's my mum. I'll stay with her."

He knew when he was beaten. I was the one with Mum when she went for the X-ray, and when the consultant showed her the pictures and pointed out where the fracture was, and said they'd want to keep her in overnight.

"I'm so sorry, Libby," she said, with her eyes filling up. "It shouldn't have happened."

"It's not your fault," I said again. "It just happened. So long as you're being looked after, that's all that matters. You just rest."

I thought over what she might need – a nightie, washing things, something to read, maybe some sweets – and we chatted and made a list. Finally I kissed her goodbye – the shock and the anaesthetic were making her tired – and went to find Gray and Cam. The hospital shop was closed but Gray had found a drinks machine and Cam was glugging one of those rocket-fuel drinks from a can.

 63

"Mum has to stay in overnight, so we need to go back to the cottage and pack a bag for her," I told them. "And I'll pack some things for myself too, so I can stay over with her."

Gray gave a kind little laugh. Only a little one, but it was still a laugh. "There's no need for you to stay," Gray said gently. "The doctor told me it's only a fracture; she doesn't need her hand holding. She'll be fine."

"I don't want her to be alone," I insisted. "She might need help with stuff, and they're always saying how busy the nurses are."

Cam was bored and probably hyped up on his fizzy drink, so he was now pulling on Gray's hand and swinging back and forwards as if he wanted to get into orbit, chanting "I hate hospitals" over and over again.

"There won't be a bed for you or anything," he went on. "The only rooms are for relations of people who really need to be there, you know, if somebody's ... really sick. They wouldn't let you stay in them."

"That's fine," I said. "I'll sleep in a chair beside Mum."

Afterwards, I thought about how Gray seemed completely familiar with hospitals, and how he knew about the rooms for people to stay in and why Cam hated hospitals, and I felt bad about it, but at the time it didn't occur to me. Gray took Cam's hand in both of his, presumably to stop Cam from dislocating his shoulder.

"We'd better get home and get this bag packed, then," he said. "Before it snows again."

I hadn't thought of that – I'd lost track of the time. We piled into the car and drove back through darkness and flying snow that I would have found exciting and dramatic if we hadn't been leaving my mum behind. Cam finally stopped shouting to the world that he hated hospitals, and by the time we got back to the cottage he was slumped asleep in his seat, his eyelashes dark against his flushed cheeks and his black dog cuddled tightly in his arms. When Gray carried him in and laid him on his bed he barely opened his eyes. Gray put a blanket over him, closed the door softly and came to talk to me while I knelt by the grate and got the fire started. I didn't bother to turn round.

"Cam's totally crashed," he said. "Libby, I know you want to be with your mum, I understand that. But if you come to the hospital we'll have to bring Cam too, and I don't want to drag him all the way there and back again. Would you pack a bag for Kate and let me take it in, and you stay here with Cam? It should only be for about" – he paused to work out the journey time in his head – "an hour and a half, two if the weather gets any fouler. I'll be back well before ten."

"OK," I said quietly. It was so very not what I wanted. I should be with Mum, he should be with Cam, but he was the only driver and it would be cruel to make Cam go out again. Gray was right, but I didn't want him to be.

"I could drive up to Mrs Chisolm and ask her to. . ." he began, but I stopped him.

"No, it's cool," I said, and even smiled to reassure

him. "We'll be fine. I'll look after Cam." I was hoping he wouldn't wake up.

"You're a star," said Gray, but everyone says that when you've done them a favour. In my mind I was chalking it up – *he owes me one*. I made coffee and packed Mum's bag while Gray put Cam into his pyjamas and tucked him up with his black dog.

"He'll sleep for hours," he said. "I doubt he'll wake up before morning. He won't know I'm gone."

I nearly said "drive safely", because it was foul out there and it was bad enough having Mum in hospital without Gray ending up in there as well and leaving me in the Arctic Circle with Kick-Off Cam for as long as it took. But I didn't want to sound like my Gran. Away went Gray, cat-hat and all like a polar explorer, and I went to check that Cam was OK.

Suddenly I realized that I could have a lovely evening of books, telly and biscuits. I could watch what I liked; I didn't have to fit in with anyone else. The fire crackled and danced with a smell of wood ash, the snow fell in soft light showers outside the window, and it was lemon bonbon time. When the fire burned low I put another log on, checked Cam again, made a hot drink, finished one book, started another. In the warmth of the fireside I was even falling asleep. The snow turning to sleet drove against the window and woke me, and I was astonished to see that it was half past nine. In this weather Gray would have to creep along the country roads, but it didn't bother me if he was late home.

Ten. Quarter past. Half past. Was this just Gray not getting his act together, or should I be worried? Probably he was just spending a bit more time with Mum.

Worry crept into me like a draught from a window. There were still flurries of sleet, the driving conditions were treacherous and Gray must be tired. It would be so easy to lose control of the car, to skid and hit something, and how long would it be before anyone found him? Would he be found in time? The more I thought about it, the more real it seemed. Who'd look after Cam? I began to wonder how long I should leave it before I rang the police.

I went to the door and listened for an engine. In the complete and smothering blackness, an owl hooted. That was all. I closed the door quietly.

When the phone rang, I jumped.

Chapter Six

It was a loud harsh ring, and I'd forgotten where the phone was. Luckily, Cam hadn't woken up by the time I found it, tucked behind the television.

"Hi, it's Libby," I said at last. It could only be Gray at the other end. At least, I hoped so. "Are you OK? How's Mum?"

"She's OK, she's comfortable," he said. "But it's been snowing non-stop here, and now it's freezing solid. I tried to get back to the cottage, but I had to turn back. The police have blocked the road; they're hoping to have it clear by morning. Libby, I'm sorry, but there's no way I can get back tonight. You'll be on your own. I hate to put you in this position, but. . ."

"It's fine, don't worry," I said, because I'd guessed what he was going to say before he said it. All I had to do was feed us, keep us warm, and look after Cam, and I'd been doing that since we arrived. I could cope. "Don't worry, there's nothing going on that I can't handle."

"I'll phone Ailsa and ask her to look in," went on Gray.

"Don't be silly," I said. What was Ailsa supposed to do, battle her way through the pitch dark and the ice with a casserole and a hot-water bottle? "There's no need to bother Ailsa. Stay where you are, and make sure the nurses are taking good care of Mum. If she wants painkillers, see that she gets them. Give her all my love. See you both tomorrow."

But as I put the phone down I wondered if I really would see them the next day. All that snow and ice between us and the hospital wasn't going to vanish overnight, whatever the police said. It might be another day or more before the roads were passable.

I checked through the cupboards and the fridge. We might run out of milk and bread, but there was plenty of everything else, and from what I'd seen of Cam he'd happily live on beans and hot chocolate. We'd be fine, just so long as Cam didn't have one of his moments – jump off the roof, or set fire to anything. I was too old to say to myself that I wanted my mum, but I couldn't help thinking how much nicer it would be if we were together by the fire, chatting and laughing about things and maybe playing some silly game. Just her and me, the way it had always been.

But no, I was in charge, in my remote little

gingerbread cottage with snow nearly up to the window sills and Cam fast asleep. All was well on my watch. *Libby's here.* I looked in on Cam and he looked inexpressibly sweet, warm, pink-cheeked and solemn in his sleep, clutching his black dog. (Then again, I suppose a little baby alligator looks cute when it's asleep.) I hoped Mum would sleep well, too. I wasn't bothered about Gray. If he hadn't insisted on one more ski run none of this would be happening. Poor Mum had fallen for "clever but clueless" again, and the thought of it made my eyes prickle. Gray was so useless, it was amazing Cam was still alive. I thought of Cam's bright-faced, pretty mother. What would she think about the way Gray was raising her son?

"I've got him," I whispered, because in the glow of Cam's night light, it felt perfectly natural to talk to her. "He's OK. I'm on it."

That night I took my duvet and the pillows into the sitting room, put up the fireguard, and settled down to sleep on the settee because the chance to sleep in a room with a real fire was too good to miss. I burrowed down under the quilt and watched the heart of the fire glowing steadily until my eyes closed.

A door banged. The house shuddered. The bit of my brain that responds to noise woke up. The rest didn't. I simply couldn't get my eyes to open, even when Cam climbed on top of me and pulled off the covers. I think I said, "Go back to bed, Cam," but it might have been "Get lost", I can't remember.

70

"Where are they?" he screamed, and he shook me hard. "Where are they?! Tell me where they are! Tell me NOW!"

In spite of everything in my mind and body telling me to go back to sleep, I sat up. There had to be a way of telling Cam that I hadn't finished sleeping, I wasn't nearly finished sleeping, and it was *really important*. He'd put the light on, so even when I did manage to get one eye open I had to shut it again.

"Where are they?" he demanded, dragging on my arm to get me up. What had I said last night? *Libby's here*. Well, maybe fifty per cent of her was, but the half that was capable of speech was still unconscious. With massive concentration and my eyes still shut, I managed to slur a few reasonable sentences together.

"You remember. My mum – Kate – she had to go into hospital. Well, your daddy took her a bag of things she might need. And then it got very, very snowy and he couldn't drive back."

I was drifting into sleep again; I couldn't help it. I forced my eyes open and squinted at my watch. What a surprise, there really is such a time as ten to four in the morning. Ten to four in the morning is like the Loch Ness Monster, something I'd heard of but never really believed existed. "It's nearly four o'clock in the morning, Cam. It's the middle of the night."

"Don't be silly, midnight is the middle of the night!" He said it much too loudly.

"Whatever. It's sleep time," I mumbled. "Go back to bed."

"Can I come in with you?" he asked.

If I'd been awake enough to argue I'd have taken him back to his own bed, black dog and all, but I wasn't up to it. I lifted a corner of the duvet and let him snuggle in. At least he didn't snore. I lay with a small elbow in my ribs and the little black dog squashed up against my shoulder. In a fuzzy sort of way I knew that, if Mum and Gray stayed together, there'd be a lot more of this. I knew it, but I wasn't sure how I felt about it. I was vaguely aware of Cam wriggling, fidgeting, rolling off the settee, getting back in and finally, thank goodness, going back to his own bed. I must have fallen asleep at last, because after that I didn't know a thing until he landed on top of me from a great height. It was daylight by then – about eightish, I think.

"They've gone out!" he yelled tearfully, and flung the quilt off me. "They've gone away by themselves! Where are they?"

He didn't remember a thing about the conversation at stupid o'clock. The poor little soul was completely confused and bewildered. I was learning that a confused Cam became a scared Cam and a scared Cam became all-hell-let-loose. He banged both fists on the settee then launched himself at me, so I held his wrists.

"Go and find them!" he screamed.

"Cam, listen," I said, and realized I'd have to wait until he was calm enough to hear me, so I stopped talking and just looked at him until he got the message and shut up. Slowly, bit by bit, I reminded him of what had happened the day before and he listened with a cross little pout across his mouth. He looked so offended and so babyish that I wanted to laugh. Bit by bit I explained that Handsome But Hopeless was stuck in hospital with several miles of impassable snow and ice between us, and finally Cam got it.

"Then, when are we going to the Wildlife Park?" he asked.

I'd almost forgotten that this was the last full day of our holiday. Flora's Wildlife Park was the only thing Cam had said he wanted to do. I still hadn't a clue when Mum and Gray would be back, let alone how we'd get home.

"We'll see if Daddy phones," I said. "Then I suppose we'll go to Flora's after they get back." It was only around three miles to Flora's. As soon as they got back I could make Mum comfortable on the settee with coffee, cake and the fire, then press the car keys into Gray's hand and tell him to get his ducks in a row. Well, you know, I wouldn't say it, but I'd think it. As the landline only took incoming calls I couldn't phone the hospital and ask after Mum, but I wished desperately that I could. I stepped outside with my phone on the off-chance that just this time, I might get a signal, that what had never worked before would work now because I wanted it so, so much – no, not a thing.

"Cam, it's time to get dressed," I said, and while he did that I sorted out some breakfast. He appeared with odd socks, asked when we could go to see the animals at Flora's, yummied down a huge bowl of cereal, asked when Daddy would be home so we could go to see the animals at Flora's, cleaned his teeth, asked me when...

Oh, mercy. It was going to be a long day.

The phone rang. Cam pounced before I could get to it.

"Hello, Dad!" he said, and in less than a second I saw all the brightness leaving his face. A subdued little Cam handed me the phone.

"A lady wants to talk to you," he said grumpily.

It was Ailsa, explaining that the road from her house was solid ice. I offered to bring the horses out and she was very grateful.

"What did the wee boy mean about his Daddy?" she asked. "Is he not there?" When I explained she offered to come down and stay with us as soon as the road was clear, but I told her we could cope.

I put the phone down and turned to Cam. Poor little soul. There was a single tear on his face. This wasn't the holiday either of us had wanted, and I hurt for him.

"Now, Cam," I said, kneeling down to get to his eye level, "Peggy and Jayjay are in their stable and they want to come out to play. Shall we go and let them out?"

We went out into the brisk, cold morning and Cam was calm and happy, gently patting Peggy and Jayjay's flanks and talking to them. He was at home with animals, perhaps because they were uncomplicated.

The snow had drifted in the field so that it lay in humps like an unmade bed. All the time we were there, Cam was quite happily absorbed in watching Peggy and Jayjay. I wasn't. I wanted to go back into the

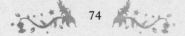

warm little house and I was beginning to find all that white-on-white just a teeny bit too much. If I'd seen a bright yellow daffodil poking through the snow I'd have been so glad to see some colour I'd have hugged and kissed it and asked it to be my best friend for ever. But Cam was enjoying being outside. We built another snowman – *If this goes on,* I thought, *they'll outnumber us, get organized and declare war on the English* – and I finally coaxed him indoors with hot chocolate. Half a hot chocolate later, he was off again.

"When are we going to Flora's to see the animals? When will we go to Flora's? They've got otters at Flora's; when will we see the otters? Is it time to go to Flora's yet? When *will* it be time?" He kept it up so long that I sorted out an early lunch in the hope of distracting him. At least it would distract *me*. I'd had a whole morning, *a whole morning,* of Cam all by myself, starting at ten to four! He'd begun by trying to beat me up and deafen me, and now if he didn't shut up I was going to have to open a window and throw him to the snowmen. I was thinking, as I made sandwiches, of taking him out on the tea-tray sledge in the afternoon. Hopefully he'd see some animals, which would make him a lot happier and give him something to tell Gray about afterwards. *Please, please, let there be ptarmigan, or a hare. Some of those shaggy Highland cows with horns like handlebars – he'd love that. Even a sheep, oh, please, even a sheep would be something so long as it's not dead and being hacked apart by crows.*

Apart from anything else, I'd have given the world

for an hour or two with a book. I was up to a really good bit, too, when Granny Weatherwax turns up with a—

There was a long, heartbroken wail like an animal in pain. I dashed out of the kitchen and found Cam running headlong to find me, his arms out and tears pouring down his face. He grabbed me so hard that I nearly fell, and had to put a hand on the wall to steady myself.

"What happened, Cam?" I knelt down and he curled up sobbing in my lap. I lifted his hair back from his forehead to check for bruises and asked him if he was hurt – had he fallen and banged his head on the hearth? Had I forgotten to put up the fireguard? A look past him into the sitting room told me that the guard was still in place, so at least he wasn't burned. I kept asking him what it was, but he just sobbed and sobbed, and every time I thought he was stopping he started again. I was kneeling on the hard floor with Cam on my lap and my feet hurting, but I couldn't move. After what seemed like for ever he hiccupped and slumped down, exhausted.

"Sweetie," I said, kissing the top of his head because it was there, "are you missing your Daddy?"

He shook his head, gave a soggy sniff, and dried his eyes with the heel of his hand. There was another hiccup before he finally got the words out.

"I wanted to see the animals." One more tear rolled down his face. I brushed it away with my thumb, planted another kiss, and held him, rocking him gently, wishing so much that I could make it all right for him and get him to Flora's. Then from the wish came the thought, and from the thought came the idea – could we do it? Could we get to Flora's on our own?

"Let's see," I said at last. I was giving myself thinking time, making it up as I went along. "There are some lovely sandwiches for lunch, and you can have tomato soup if you like. I can't eat it all by myself so I think you'd better help."

I went back to the kitchen to heat up the soup, and called Cam when it was ready. There wasn't a sound. I went to find him, and the whole house was quieter than it should have been.

The door was open. There was Cam, in his jacket and wellies, pulling the sledge along behind him, heading for the trees.

"Lunchtime!" I called cheerfully, wondering what I was going to do if he refused to come back.

"I'm going to see some animals," said Cam.

"What a good idea!" I said. "But it's a bit cold just now, isn't it? Shall we have some soup first?"

He enjoyed his lunch when he finally sat down to it, but all the time he was looking out of the window, and when I left him just for a moment I found him with his coat back on. He was determined to get out.

It was still a clear day. When I'd finished and he was carefully nibbling off the chocolate round the edge of a biscuit, I sorted out some of Gray's touristy stuff and a map, and spread them all out on the floor.

"Please, please, can we see some animals?" he begged. There were tears in his eyes.

Flora's Wildlife Centre was, as I said, only three

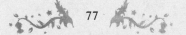

miles away. That was probably too far for Cam to walk, but we had the tea-tray sledge. In my head I began to work out how long it would take us to get to the Wildlife Centre.

I took another look at the maps, then fetched Cam's coat and some of his socks, and put them on the fireguard to warm. Cam helped himself to another biscuit while glancing sideways at me to see if I'd noticed, and I pretended not to. If he was more interested in biscuits than in what I was doing that was fine with me, especially as I didn't exactly know what I was doing myself. I packed biscuits, fruit and sweets, cartons of orange juice and a torch in case it got dark before we were back. Cam was going to Flora's Wildlife Centre if it killed me. I'd just seen that poor little scrap break his heart over it. Over the last twenty-four hours Gray had put Mum in danger and left Cam and me to look after ourselves, or rather, me to look after Cam, so that's what I'd do. Cam was a right little pain in the whatnot, but he was also a disappointed little boy. His mum might be dead and his dad wasn't there, but he had me.

I rammed my phone into my bag in case we found anywhere in this Siberian wilderness with a signal. Cam would have his day out.

Was I doing it only for Cam's sake? Really and truly, was it only because I couldn't bear to see him miserable, or because I simply couldn't stand him whining on any longer? Or was this just the nearest I could get to giving Gray a slap and a shake for not spending enough time with Cam, and putting my mum in danger – at least, that was how it had seemed to me at the time. Maybe a bit of all those, but above all I wanted to do this for Cam. I'm quite sure of that.

I sat down beside him and he looked at me with those huge dark eyes. Half a biscuit was sticking out of his mouth.

"Now, Cam, listen to me," I said. "We're going out with the sledge."

"The chee chay?" he asked.

"The tea tray, and don't talk with your mouth full. We're going to follow the road as far as we can and see what we can see and I'll *try* – I can't promise anything, but I'll *try* – to get us to the Wildlife Centre."

He said nothing, but stars glowed in his eyes. He nodded.

"Remember, I can't promise," I repeated. "We might not get there. If the snow gets too bad or we have another storm we'll have to turn back at once, and no arguing. And by the time we get there we won't have long, but we can have a little look." I reckoned that Cam didn't have much idea of time. Depending on the snow, we should get a couple of hours there. I remembered something that Granny used to get me to do when she'd explained something.

"Now, Cam," I said, "can you tell me what I just told to you, so I know you've understood?"

He did, and after a couple of attempts I knew he'd got it. At the last minute I decided to leave a note in case Mum and Gray got back before us:

Off to Wildlife Park, see you soon –
Libby and Cam xx

I damped down the fire, put the guard back, checked everything was turned off, and made sure Cam was so wrapped up he was almost circular. I put a spare pair of his socks in my bag in case his feet got wet, because Mum used to do that for me when I was little. I thought it might help both of us if he had a chance for a run before he went on the sledge, so off we went under high blue skies, leaping like hurdlers over the mounds of glittering snow and I swear you could have put us on a Christmas card.

If I'd known how things would all work out, would I have done it anyway?

I don't know. But I'm glad I did.

Chapter Seven

I'd told Cam we'd be more likely to see some wild animals if we were quiet, so once he was on the tray he sat there with his mouth firmly shut and as still as if he wanted to be taken for a stone. If he'd turned blue I wouldn't have known if he was hypothermic or just holding his breath. This meant that I had to be silent, too. If I said anything I could feel him scowling at my back without even looking round. It made me want to laugh out loud, but I mustn't. Winding Cam up would be so easy it wouldn't be fair.

And the walk was just beautiful – such clear sky and gleaming snow that I wished I'd brought sunglasses. There were painted poles on either side of the road so that you could find the way in snowdrifts, so this weather must have been normal up there. We were passing the trees when Cam whispered, "Squirrel!"

It was, too! I was delighted that Cam saw it first. There was a flash of chestnut red as it ran up the tree, disappeared, and then came round again from the other side. A bird overhead might have been a buzzard or even an eagle, I don't know, and we squinted against the brightness as it wheeled away from us. Soon after that we came to a junction that looked familiar from when we first arrived, which seemed like months ago.

I checked the map. We had to take the single-track road, which went through the pine forest. There was less snow here because of the trees, but just enough to run the tea tray. It wasn't so easy because the ground was bumpier, but Cam didn't fall off or complain.

According to the map this was a long road that led round a bend and up a hill, then back on to the main road, or as main as the roads got around here. Cam must have used up his being-very-quiet allowance for the day because he was pointing at things and asking questions. In the shadow of the trees there was no more glare from the snow, which made it easier to notice details – the slide of snow from a branch, tracks of birds' feet, a shape that might have been a slender tree trunk, or might be…

I stopped and looked more carefully. At first glance it looked like a stem of something and a shadow in the trees, but I watched to see if it moved.

"Why have—" began Cam.

"Shh!" I said. Moving as smoothly as I could I crouched down beside Cam and pointed at what I thought might be a deer.

"From this tree nearest to us, count five back," I

said. "Now four along." It wasn't easy for him to work out because trees don't grow in exactly straight lines, but then the deer took a few steps forward and turned its head. I think it knew we were there. It was almost as if it was looking at something just above us.

From the tight little gasp, I knew that Cam had seen it. Without even looking at him, I knew that his eyes were shining like candles in a church. Moving very gently, he knelt up on the tray. "A deer!" he whispered.

It had no antlers, just a small, elegant head on a powerful chestnut body. Its ears twitched. But the spell couldn't last for ever. Its hearing must have been pin-sharp. Its ears flicked, and with a blur of white rump it was away, making a fast, sure path through the forest, leaving us watching until it was out of sight. We might not make it to Flora's but we'd seen a deer, and what's more, we'd seen it in the wild. It was part of the landscape. Flora's was run by people, but in the wild it's the landscape and the animals that make the rules, and sometimes, just for a very short time, we get to join in. This was one of those moments, and Cam and I had shared it together.

"That was so special!" I said as I stood up, stretched the stiffness out of my legs, and picked up the rope again. All that time I'd been keeping still my toes had begun to hurt with cold. I was about to ask Cam if he was ready to move, and then he screamed.

I jumped. Shock ran through the forest. Birds flapped out of rustling treetops, there was a quick, quiet whisk of things running, and all the time Cam went on screaming and pointing – it was terrifying. I tried to hold him and talk to him but he pushed me away with both hands and went on pointing, only drawing breath for another scream. I tried to follow the line of his arm, but he was shaking and I had no idea what he was trying to show me.

"Stop screaming and tell me what it is," I said firmly, and then again, "Be quiet, Cam. Tell me."

I don't think he heard me but then I turned my head and I very nearly screamed, too. It was the dead body of the wildcat.

It lay curled on its side, as still as granite, half in and half out of a hollow in a tree as if it had been trying to crawl out. Even though I knew it was dead, I was wary and needed to check. I put out a finger to touch the tip of its ear, then, when there was no flicker of movement, felt for a pulse. It was cold and lifeless, and Cam's cries rang past like a lament.

The wildcat had something in its mouth, and I thought it had died while hunting. I'm not squeamish, but I had to kind of pull myself together before I looked more carefully to see what it was holding.

Oh. Oh no, no. The kitten was like a tiny version of its mother, its eyes shut, peaceful, like Cam in his sleep. I touched it, but I already knew that it was stiff and frozen. I saw it, I wanted to cry. What could I tell Cam? That not only the cat, but her kitten too, lay dead in the snow? Better that he didn't know.

I stood up, and my legs were a bit shaky. Cam was running out of steam and the screams were thinner,

but he ran at me and went for me with all the strength of his boots and fists. I dropped to my knees, grabbed him, and held him as still as I could.

"You killed the wildcat!" he yelled, fighting with all his strength to get free. "You killed it! You're evil! You murdered it! You're a murderer, I'm telling my dad! I'm telling your mum! Let me go! You're a witch, I hate you, I hate you, you witch!" He stopped, but only because he was thinking of worse things to call me. "You cow! You stupid fat cow! Stupid fat smelly cow!"

When he started on "cow" I'd had enough of kneeling in freezing snow. Quite enough.

"Be quiet and listen to me, Cameron," I said, so sternly that I must have surprised him. He muttered something rude under his breath but he stopped shouting and trying to kill me. Maybe calling him "Cameron" made the difference.

"Now listen," I repeated. "I did not kill the wildcat. Cats do not die just because you throw a bit of snow or an apple at them. Do you understand? The apple didn't even touch it."

"Did the snow hit it?" he asked

"I've no idea, but it wouldn't do it any harm. It was less than a snowball. The cat was used to snow; it lived in it all the time."

I could feel the tension leave his body as he accepted this. We both relaxed.

"I should think it was the cold," I said. "It was bitterly cold last night, and stormy. I think she died of cold."

Or hunger, but I didn't want to tell Cam that. He'd be terribly distressed. I didn't want to tell him about the kitten for the same reason.

The kitten? Oh, stupid, stupid me! Since when did a cat have only one kitten? Grandpa would have thought of it immediately. There must be more of her litter back there in the forest.

"I have to go back to her," I said. "Just for a moment or two."

"I want to come with you." He looked at me with that straight, determined mouth. *Give me strength!* Now what was I supposed to do? I looked into his eyes.

"You can come if you want to," I said, speaking very slowly and clearly to make sure it went in. "But if you do, you're going to see something very sad. *Very* sad. And you must promise not to scream. You absolutely must not scream." That might have been a bit much to ask, but I'd had enough of Cam's hysterics for one day. Hand in hand, we went back to the wildcat. From the way she was curled round, I think she had been trying to protect the kitten with the warmth of her own body for as long as she could.

"This cat was a mummy cat with kittens," I explained. "She had this kitten in her mouth because that's what mummy cats do to pick up their children." I imagined her venturing out into the snow to bring this wandering kitten back to safety and succumbing to the cold at the same time. No wonder she'd gone for us so viciously. She'd been protecting her young, as all animals do.

As carefully as I could I opened the cat's mouth, and the kitten dropped to the ground, not moving. It was old enough to have fur. Poor mother cat, how could she find enough in this harsh winter to feed herself, especially when she had a litter needing milk? Most wild animals, including wildcats, have litters in spring, but this one must have given birth early. I felt my eyes fill as I ran a hand over the thick, coarse coat.

"Are you crying?" asked Cam.

"I'm sad about the cat," I said, putting it as simply as I could. Then Cam, who had just been kicking me with all his strength and fury, put his hand over mine.

"It's all right," he said solemnly. "Don't cry."

Bless him! He was talking to me the way he talked to the horses.

"Thank you," I said. "You're a kind boy. Now, the thing is, Cam, cats don't usually have just one kitten."

"They have litters," he said.

"Yes, they have litters," I agreed. "So we have to check if she had any more kittens, and whether any of them are alive."

I took out the torch and shone it into the hollow tree. There was some dried grass and thin, scraggy-looking fur – rabbit, probably – which must have been bedding. No kittens. The cat's body still lay where I had seen it, and I slipped my hand against her belly.

Yes. Two kittens were still nestled against her, snuggled so closely that I would never have seen them. The first one I lifted out was warm, but hung limply in my hand without a pulse. When I reached in again, something moved underneath my hand. I caught my breath.

Something was living; a heart was beating under my fingers. My heartbeat quickened. Under the coarse coat, a live kitten was still trying to suckle from its mother.

As gently as I could, I lifted it out. Hardly the size of my hand, it blinked at me and opened its mouth to let out a hiss like the opening of a bottle. Feebly it flexed tiny, needle-sharp claws. It was afraid and in danger of dying from cold and hunger, but so far, it had survived. Frightened and defensive, it reminded me of Cam.

"That one's alive!" said Cam.

"Yes, Cam, it is." Bracing myself against the sudden cold I took off one of my gloves and slipped the kitten into it. The top of its head showed over the top.

"Are you going to keep it?" he asked.

"It needs help," I told him. "It's only a baby and it needs a warm place and milk like its mother's milk, and people who know how to look after it. And the best place for that..." Cam was staring at the kitten as if nothing else existed in the world. "Are you hearing this, Cam? The best place for that is Flora's Wildlife Centre, and that's where we're going. They'll know what to do."

All this time I'd had half a mind on turning back if the weather got worse. But it could be the difference between life and death for the kitten.

"Will you be his mummy?"

"It needs a cat mummy," I said. "They might be able to find one but we need to keep it warm till we get there."

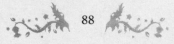

88

"It's not *it*, it's *him*," Cam insisted. I hadn't a clue what it was, but if Cam wanted to think it was male, that was fine with me.

"Keeping him warm will be your job," I said. "You have to hold him closely so that he can feel your warmth. Shall we tuck him into your coat?"

Cam nodded with that bright eyed look. He was loving this. I don't think anyone had ever given him responsibility before.

"I'll be his daddy," he said, and he stood still while I tucked the kitten, still in my glove, inside his padded jacket. He clapped both hands over the little bulge. "Hasn't he got a real daddy?" he asked, and I managed not to laugh.

"Cat daddies don't stay around for long," I told him. "Mostly they leave the little ones with the mums."

"Is that what your dad did?" he asked, and I pretended not to hear.

With my gloved hand pulling the sledge and the other in my pocket I set off again, walking more quickly than before – and not just because I wanted to get the kitten to Flora's as soon as possible.

It had been shady under the trees but now that we had stepped back on to the path I could see the sky was overcast, not as bright as it had been. Dark clouds were above us, and we still had a long way to go. I strode off at the best pace I could, determined not to look at the gathering clouds as the first flakes fell and a breeze rustled the forest.

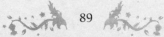

Chapter Eight

"It's snowing again!" yelled Cam from the sledge. "Isn't it exciting!"

Yes it was – the snow twirled softly around us, and even though I was worried about the kitten, I was loving being in this fairy-tale picture. The quiet magic of white winter was all around us and we were a part of the picture. We were journeying through a Hansel and Gretel forest on a mission to save one tiny life, and I was pulling the sledge like some pioneering heroine.

"When will we get there?" asked Cam.

"As soon as we can!" I called back.

"How soon is that?"

"When it is," I said, and at that point he must finally have realized he was on a hiding to nothing, asking me questions I couldn't answer. But it must have been further than it looked on the map. The cold was getting to my feet, and the effort of pulling the sledge was harder work where the snow was thinner. But we had to go on. I had no idea how long the kitten could live without milk.

The road began to slope uphill, only a little, but pulling the sledge was harder. The snowflakes were thicker, more and more, and the wind grew fiercer.

"Cam," I called, "would you like to walk for a bit?"

I was afraid that he'd go into Grumpy Goblin mode, but he was fine. He plodded bravely through the snow beside me with one hand clamped over the small bulge of kitten under his jacket. I picked up the tray to hold in front of him, and we lowered our heads against the storm, keeping as close as we could to the trees.

"Will the kitten miss his mummy?" asked Cam.

I suspected that this might become Cam's Question of the Day, or of the afternoon, at least. "I think he'll be happy as long as he has someone to feed him and keep him warm," I said. "A human mummy."

"Has his mummy gone to heaven?"

How should I know? I'm OK with the idea of heaven. I hope there is one. But with wildcats in it?

"I'm sure she is," I said, and added, "but in heaven she'll be a nice, good cat and won't hurt anyone." I didn't want Cam imagining his own mum in heaven being savaged by a wildcat. "Everyone's nice in heaven." Then, as I felt we were getting into deep water with all this, I changed the subject. "He's a very lucky kitten to have you looking after him," I said.

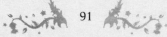

"He likes me," said Cam happily, and then we both swayed as a vicious blast of wind whooshed down and nearly pushed us off our feet. Snow dropped from the trees. We were wearing hats and scarves, but all the same I felt something nastily cold and wet going down the back of my neck. As the chill spread through my spine and into my ribs, Cam laughed and pointed.

"You've got a snow hat!" he said.

"So have you!" I called back, and the Libby he could see grinned and laughed with him while the Libby inside me panicked at the icy cold down the back of my neck, and the long walk behind us, and the long walk ahead which suddenly seemed far too long, and the snow, and whose stupid idea was this anyway? Oh, yes, mine. Snowflakes were landing on Cam's eyelashes. All around us, the landscape became sheets on a washing line, overlapping until I couldn't tell one shape from another.

"Let's press on, Cam," I said. "Imagine we're walking on the moon."

This time, he was happy to pretend. He strode ahead with one arm stretched out to the side, pretending to space-hop over craters while the other hand stayed firmly over his jacket where the kitten lay. At this point I was holding the tray over his head like an umbrella, and it was soon inches deep with snow, glistening like icing. Ahead of us, barely visible through the blizzard, was a road sign. We were nearly at the crossing.

"We're getting there, Cam," I said. "Do you want a ride to the crossroads?"

"No thanks!" he shouted. "I'm walking on the moon!"

Cam wasn't just behaving reasonably, he was being exceptionally *nice*. He was pleasant to be with. Was this what it took to bring out the best in him – snowstorms and a homeless kitten? Then he said something and I hadn't really been listening, and had to ask him to repeat it.

"I have to look after the kitten," he said solemnly.

"You certainly do," I said, hoping the poor thing was still alive. "You're doing it really well."

"We'll run!" he said, but we couldn't, not very far. The wind had risen. The going was much harder now and my legs hurt, but eventually, cold to the bones, we reached the junction. I was relieved to see it. There wouldn't be far to go after that, just a little way and a bit of a hill. It wasn't likely that there'd be anything on the road unless it was a lost Highland cow, or a snowplough, but all the same I got Cam to stop and check before we crossed. Then we stepped out from the shelter of the forest, and the blizzard swept down on us without mercy, like a charge.

If I hadn't ducked and grabbed Cam we'd both have been knocked to the ground. Out in the open there was nothing between us and the sheer wildness of a Highland blizzard that we could hardly stand up against, let alone walk through. Snow drove into my eyes and I wrapped myself round Cam, trying to look up, blinking and squinting against the storm. I had to get us under a tree, though I didn't know if I could move without losing my balance.

"Over here, Cam!" I yelled, trying to steer him to the trees, but he resisted.

"There's a house!" he was shouting. "There's a little house!"

"Where?"

I narrowed my eyes as the wind bit into my face. Cam was pointing to the other side of the road, away from the direction we needed to go. Set back from the road was some kind of a shelter, not a house at all, just some kind of a stone shed that must have been there for shepherds or something. There was no door in the doorway, but at least it had four walls and a roof, and I didn't resist as Cam grabbed my sleeve and dragged me towards it. The gale was throwing us in the right direction, and we stumbled in.

Two blankets were rolled up in a corner, but they looked old and grimy and I didn't want to touch them. Nothing else was there except a battered old fire basket – you know, the kind that looks like a metal waste-paper basket on legs – with a bit of grey ash in the bottom, and a heap of dried leaves blown in by the wind. The floor was earth, but there was nothing else to sit on. I knelt down and tried to pull Cam on to my lap, but he wriggled up again.

"You can make a fire in there!" he said.

"We haven't any matches," I said. I hadn't brought any with me – how was I to know we'd need to light a fire? I wasn't doing a Duke of Edinburgh's Award. Cam was gazing all around us.

"What's that?" he asked.

I stood up, stamped warmth into my feet and rubbed my hands together. High on the wall above the top of my head was a rough wooden shelf.

Oh, please! I thought, and reached up. My hand closed on the hard coldness of a metal box, and I lifted it down and opened it. *Yes.* Inside was a battered old box of matches. There weren't many in there, but at least the box had kept them dry.

The leaves looked dry enough for kindling, but we hadn't any wood. Keeping the box of matches in my hand in case Cam took a liking to them, I went outside, turned my back to the wind, and found a couple of fallen branches. They were soaking, but they were all I had and at least I could try. I got Cam to pile leaves into the fire basket and he was on it at once, scooping them up in his free hand and piling them in, all the time keeping the other hand over his jacket where the kitten was. When he'd done that I shoved a branch on top and set light to the leaves.

Cam stared with fascination as the flames tasted the kindling. There was a touch of warmth and a bright flare of orange as the leaves curled, but it was no good. The wet wood smouldered and went out, the leaves burnt away, and we were left with smoke in our eyes and a few sticks poking sullenly out of the basket. Oh well, it had been nice while it lasted. There had been a brief touch of warmth on our fingers and faces before it died out all together.

"Why didn't it work?" asked Cam.

"Because the wood was too wet," I told him, and

I put the matches back on the shelf where I'd found them. *Because I'm out of my depth now and I couldn't get it right.* I sat Cam on my lap again and this time he didn't object. He looked down the front of his coat.

"He's all right," he said. The kitten opened its eyes, wriggled a bit, and went back to sleep, which seemed like a good idea to me.

"You've done well there, Cam," I said. "You've kept him safe." *Which is more than I've done for you,* I thought, *now that we're stranded with no signal.*

No signal? I might as well try the phone. All the time we'd been moving, the need to keep going had kept my mind off the cold. Now it was worse, eating into my fingers and toes. I took out my phone and dropped it because my hands were frozen into clumsiness. I could hardly manage the keypad, and when I tried, there was still no signal. Of course there wasn't. I hadn't expected one, but I had to try.

Suddenly, it was too much. I squeezed my eyes shut. *If only I hadn't started this. I could give all my heart to turn back time and have Cam and I stay in the cottage, by the fire, and...*

Cam was watching me curiously. "Are you all right?" he asked.

I opened my eyes and smiled. "Yes, are you?"

"I'm a bit cold," he said. I laughed, and he frowned at me.

"I'm not laughing at you, Cam," I said quickly. I knew I wasn't speaking very clearly, because my mouth was too cold to work properly. "It's just that it's freezing; it's like the South Pole. We're like a pair of icicles and you just say you're a bit cold. It's called understatement." *Funny little Cam,* I thought. "Cuddle in tight. You keep the little cat warm and I'll keep you warm. It's a good thing we've got lots of winter clothes on."

"The kitten's keeping me warm," he said. He was stroking its head very gently with his fingertip. I folded my arms more closely round him, resting my cheek on the top of his head. Presently he asked for a drink, and I fumbled with cold fingers for the little cartons of orange juice. I didn't want one – it would only make me colder inside – but Cam seemed to enjoy his. We ate chocolate biscuits that were so cold I could hardly taste the chocolate, and as I hugged Cam in close again I thought of his lovely, smiley mum. If she was looking down at us I owed her an explanation for all this.

"When will we go on?" asked Cam.

"Not yet," I said. Not with the wind outside howling like an angry ghost in a story. "When the storm stops."

"When will that be?"

"I don't know. When you do you think it will be?"

"I don't know."

"Neither do I," I said.

"Soon?"

"Maybe."

"Are there any more biscuits?"

At least I could say yes to that. There were crisps and squished bananas too, and he had quite a little picnic before announcing that he needed a wee.

"Go round the back of the hut," I said. "Nobody will see you. Shall I hold the kitten?"

I don't think he wanted to hand it over, but he could see the sense of it. It was still tucked into my glove like a small teddy bear in a Christmas stocking, and he laid it gently in my hands and ran outside. I only hoped the wind wouldn't snatch him up and carry him out to sea.

The kitten's eyes were tightly shut as if it had made up its mind not to know what was going on. Sensible cat, that. I held it against the warmth of my neck.

"Hold on," I whispered. "You're wild, you're stronger than you look, and you have to stay alive. You know how to do that." At least, I hoped it did. There was a chilly patch on my lap where Cam had been and I was glad when he came running back.

"I melted snow!" he said with satisfaction. "There was steam coming up." It wasn't that funny really, but it seemed like it and we both got the giggles. When I put the kitten back into his cupped hands, it opened its mouth wide and made a rough little noise at the back of its throat. Cam glanced anxiously up at me.

"Is he all right?" he asked.

"Probably just missing his mum," I said, but I didn't know anything about kittens, and how often they needed to feed or whether they're supposed to sound like that. "Snuggle him up again."

I unzipped my jacket so I could pull it round Cam and give him another layer of warmth. Wrapped up together, huddling down as small as we could, we put our heads down and waited as birds and wild animals do, and I finally knew what the Highlands had been trying to teach me. Wild places have their own rules. They are the rules the animals live by, because this is their place. If you go into the wild you have to live by those rules. They don't make allowances for visitors. Bow your head to the winter and the land. Show respect.

Walking in the cold had taken every scrap of my strength, but keeping still in it was harder. Kneeling on the earth floor was like wearing ice, breathing ice, becoming ice, and every breath I took drew the winter further inside me, into my veins. I rubbed Cam's arms, trying to get a little more warmth into us both. My face stung. The bite of cold had fastened on to my bones. They were ice bones. I was held up by ice, turning into ice.

Too late, I knew that I should have kept us moving. I should have got Cam to jump up and down; we should have run from wall to wall or danced. But now it felt too late for that. I couldn't move. It was all I could do to chafe Cam's arms and legs or curl my hands over his, or speak. Harsh King Winter had gripped us, and was holding us tight. Even turning my head was an effort, and when I did, when I looked at the doorway, I could see nothing but white on white on white. There was no telling the falling snow from the road, the road from the forest, the forest from the sky.

"I wish we could go," sighed Cam. I pulled my jacket more tightly round him.

"Let's think," I said. "Let's think of something warm. If we imagine it really hard, we might feel it."

"My kitten's warm," he said. At least that meant it was alive.

"I'm going to imagine a hot bath," I said.

"Hot chocolate," said Cam.

"Or that lovely fire in the cottage," I suggested. Strangely, I discovered that if I tried hard I could imagine myself a tiny bit warmer, or at least not so cold, but I was too frozen to concentrate on anything for long. Cam wriggled back against me.

"I think my mum used to do this," he said.

"Do what?"

"Hug me in her coat," said Cam. "I think she did. I might have remembered it wrong." He went quiet for a moment or two, then carried on. "It was blue. It might not have been a coat. It smelt of hospital, and hospitals smell all horrible."

"Maybe it was her dressing gown," I said, and by this time my voice was low with cold. I wriggled my toes because that would keep the circulation going. "Wiggle your toes, Cam; it'll help them get warm."

A gust of wind roared past us, so hard and fierce that even though we were inside, I ducked. Through the gaping doorway, flakes of snow blew in. Cam squirmed round to look up at me.

"What was that noise?"

"Just the wind," I said. "Don't worry about it."

The wind was furious now and shrieking like a wild ghost, sounding as if it would go on for ever. It made my heart turn to stone inside me. We had challenged this place. We had ventured out and not been afraid

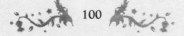

of it, and now it was punishing us. Punishing us with chill and ice and blizzard. Trees creaked as if they were in pain. Darkness would fall, and then what would happen?

It occurred to me that singing something might help but I couldn't bring a song into my head, not a single one – except for Christmas carols, of all things, and why would I want to sing about the Bleak Midwinter? *If we get out of this in one piece, I'm going to learn some songs.*

I tightened my grip round Cam. It would be all right because it had to be. That was what I told myself.

If there is anyone up there, please, please, help us. Look at us. Stop the storm. Send us help. Another gust shrieked past us and I wanted to shriek back at it, to defy it, to tell it to leave us alone. *Cam's mum, please, can you see us? Can you help us? Cam needs you!*

I shut my eyes and found that I was rocking. I don't suppose I was doing it to comfort Cam. I think I was just rocking to warm myself, or for comfort. Almost too cold to move at all, I curled and uncurled my fingers, and they hurt so badly. *Keep moving, keep moving.*

"Wriggle your fingers and toes," I told Cam, but the chilling of my face made me stammer. "We need to move, even just a little bit."

"I can't move my kitten hand," he said. It made me smile.

"Wiggle your feet, then."

At least Cam must be warmer than I was, or I hoped he was. I imagined Mum's hand on mine, a warm hand,

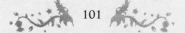

but I had to stop because this wasn't a good time to get weepy.

I tried hard not to think the word "hypothermia", but it crept in with the cold. I wondered what hypothermia felt like, and how long it took to set in. I'd left Mum and Gray a note to say where we were going, so if they were back, they'd think we were safe at Flora's. They wouldn't worry or look for us.

Even the effort of rubbing Cam's arms was becoming too tiring. Thinking was too much of an effort. So I stopped thinking.

A shout made me jolt and gasp. I'd been falling asleep, and as I came to myself it took me a few seconds to remember that I was in a stone hut.

Something felt wrong. I was colder than ever. A weight had gone. Where was Cam?

I yelled his name and tried to stand, but my legs were so numb that they wouldn't move at all. It took two or three attempts to get to my feet, and the effort made me so dizzy that I buckled and fell. With pressure ringing in my ears I called him again.

"Cam! Cam, where are you?"

I was struggling to get up again when he appeared in the doorway, shivering but smiling. His hands were still clasped to the top of his jacket, where the kitten was.

"I had to go for a wee again," he said. "And I found some wood, look!"

He was jiggling about from one foot to the other in excitement with a big smile on his face as if nothing at all was wrong. Very slowly, taking deep breaths, I

managed to stand, but my legs hurt so much that I had to turn my face away from Cam so that he wouldn't see me. Then the pins and needles set in, and it was only after they wore off that I waddled painfully to the door. Now that I wasn't cuddling Cam, I was colder than ever.

"It's here, look, it's here!" he said.

The wind had dropped, the daylight was fading, and instead of a storm, only a few light snowflakes drifted carelessly from the sky like leftovers. I followed the way Cam was pointing.

At the back of the hut where we'd never have seen it from the road, a heap of logs had been neatly stacked under a tarpaulin. I could see the long shapes piled up, and the damp ends of the ones on the bottom. I shut my eyes and leaned against the wall. *Oh, good! Next time I'm stranded in a shepherd's hut in a blizzard I'll know where to find firewood.* If only I'd gone for a wee as well, I might have discovered it.

"We can light a fire now!" announced Cam brightly.

I didn't laugh in case I upset him. "No time for that," I said with my teeth chattering. "Now that the storm's over, we can get the kitten to Flora's."

"Isn't this exciting!" said Cam. I gave up trying to understand him. If this was exciting I didn't want exciting, I wanted dead-boring ordinary. But it would be best to speak Cam's language for now.

"It's a great adventure, isn't it!" I said, as cheerfully as my frozen mouth could manage. "Now let's get moving."

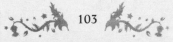

103

The wind was still in our faces, but nothing like so harsh as it had been. There was no question of pulling the sledge up that hill and Cam was a bit whingy about that, but I just told him that the sledge would slow us down and we had to hurry to get the kitten to safety. After that he tried to run ahead, skidded, and would have fallen flat if I hadn't caught him. I couldn't bear him to fall. Never mind Cam, the kitten could get hurt. And I couldn't bear another of Cam's screaming outbursts.

We tried to walk along the side of the road, but the ice was so sheer it was like trying to walk up a down escalator. At the back of my mind something was telling me that when all this was over we still had to get back to the cottage, but that problem could wait. For the moment, I didn't even know how we'd get up the hill. There was a narrow ditch, and on the other side of it the snow looked thick and soft.

"We need to get over there," I told Cam. We slithered to the side of the road where I swung him over the ditch, then jumped across to join him. Walking here was easier; we just had to pick our way through the snowdrifts. Cam wouldn't hold my hand because now he insisted on holding both hands over the kitten, so I plodded in front, my boots sinking deep into the snow, my head down and my hands in my pockets.

"Do you know about Good King Wenceslas?" I called back to Cam. "He left great big footprints—"

Below me, something gave way.

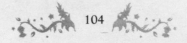

Chapter Nine

There was nothing there and my foot went down and down. I put all my weight on my other leg but my balance was going and I clutched at handfuls of reeds, or heather, or nothing, trying to save myself, stumbling sideways in the snow as icy water gripped my leg and dragged at me. With one gloved hand Cam grabbed my shoulder and for one terrifying moment I was afraid I'd pull him down too, but then I managed to get one knee and two hands on firm ground. The firm ground was under at least six inches of snow and I was soaked to the elbows, but I was safe.

"It's the ditch," I said, gasping with the sudden shock. "It must be wider along here." I caught hold of what turned out to be heather under the snow and hauled my leg out of the ditch. Heather is tough stuff, it holds on tight. Gritting my teeth, cursing quietly – I think I even growled – I scrabbled and dragged my way up and on to both knees.

This is too much. This is the worst, soaked and sprawling on my hands and knees in the snow like a beaten-up tramp. Snow was melting in my sleeves. My boots squelched with icy ditch water, the hand without a glove was scratched from the rough heather, and the cold was crueller than ever.

"You said a bad word," said Cam.

"Sorry," I whispered. Cold and pain had made me breathless. "I shouldn't have done that."

After a few deep breaths, I stood up. My right ankle hurt a little, but not too badly, I must have just turned it a bit when I fell. I curled my toes. *Squelch. Slop. Oh, yuck.* Well, now we knew that we were a tad too near the ditch. I found a fallen branch of a tree and prodded it through the snowdrifts.

Cam made a sort of . . . a sort of squeak, I suppose, as if he wanted to scream but didn't dare let it out. I turned to see him white-faced, his lips tightly folded, pointing to my hand.

I must have cut myself as I grabbed at whatever I could find. It was only a little cut, just teeny red dots, but I knew what Cam was like about blood. Part of me wanted to tell him not to make a fuss, but I could see that he was trying *very hard* not to make a fuss; he was keeping the storm tightly inside himself, turning pale and biting his lip. What sort of an effort did that demand from him? I rubbed my hand on my jacket.

"Teeny tiny cut," I said as cheerfully as I could. "It's all clean now. Come on, we've got a kitten to rescue. Quick march!"

Quick march? Where had I got that from? No chance. Slow plod, then. I wanted to hurry ahead before my wet trousers froze to my legs, but the only way was to go on patiently, one freezing measured step after the next, pushing the branch into the drifts ahead of us, Cam planting his footsteps in mine. I lifted my face to the wind and I'll swear it spat in my eyes.

"Bring it on," I muttered. I couldn't get much colder or wetter now. And Cam was being really good – he hadn't complained since the bottom of the hill.

"You're being so brave, Cam," I called back to him.

"Yes, I'm brave," he said. "I'm a hero."

"And a cat rescuer," I told him. "Cam the Cat Rescuer."

"Cam the Cat Rescuer," he repeated, and I could hear him saying it under his breath as he marched along, *Cam the Cat Rescuer,* rhythmically, over and over. It got into my brain like an earworm and I found I was marching in time to it as my wet trousers clung round my legs:

Cam the Cat Rescuer – Do you see that, you evil vicious wind? Look at us, you can't – *Cam the Cat Rescuer* – stop us, you may be the evil breath of a mammoth frozen in a – *Cam the Cat Rescuer* – polar ice cap, but you won't stop Libby and *Cam the Cat Rescuer,* and every plod was taking us one step further up the – *Cam the Cat Rescuer* – hill.

I stopped to get my breath and looked down to see how far we'd come. That was when I realized how dark it was getting. I hunted through my backpack for the torch.

"Can I hold it?" asked Cam eagerly.

"You'd have to let go of the kitten," I said shortly. I reckoned Cam was safer with the cat than the torch, and fortunately he preferred the kitten. As we'd stopped, it seemed like a good time to check on it.

Cam opened the collar of his jacket. The tiny curl of kitten was warm, and I could still feel a pulse. It was sure to be hungry, but it was still alive.

"Stay with us," I said. "Nearly there." Feeling my touch, it turned its head and fastened its mouth round my finger. With surprisingly strong little jaws, it tried to suck.

"It's hungry," I said. "We need to get moving. You're doing really, really well, Cam."

I'd almost forgotten that the original idea of all this was to give Cam his day out at Flora's. Never mind "let's see the little otters and the deer and things". It was all about the kitten, a half-starved scrap of fur that would have been dead by now if we hadn't found it. We put our heads down against a savage blast of wind and trudged on as the road veered to the right.

Suddenly there was a bit of shelter, and the road wasn't so steep. Again I stopped to get my breath back, straightened my back, and looked up.

There it was, just ahead of us! A long metal fence. A light. A sign. We were there!

"Look, Cam!" I said. "This is it!"

Cam looked. "Where are the animals?" he asked.

Oh, Cam. I took a deep breath and counted to ten. I'd finally got him to civilization and he expected a personal greeting from an elk. Preferably one in a kilt. I forced the cheerfulness into my voice.

"We have to find the way in first," I said. "Can you help me?"

It took a bit of finding, but after a bit of going one way and then another and a lot of standing on tiptoe, I found a sign pointing to the main entrance. Shivering, because the cold from my wet clothes was seeping into my bones, I bent down to him.

"We'll soon be inside, Cam," I said.

"We'll soon be inside," he echoed. I thought at first that he was just repeating himself as he often did, but when I looked down I saw that his head was bent and he was talking to the kitten even though he couldn't see it. The ground was still icy, so we picked our way along the fence. At the end was a car park and a sign pointing the way to a wooden cabin that somehow didn't look quite right.

No, no, it couldn't be. It mustn't. For Cam's sake, it mustn't be. This was more than either of us could bear.

I saw a padlocked gate. The wooden hut beside it had closed doors, and the shutters were down. I went up to it and read the sign on the door:

RECEPTION OPEN

APRIL TO OCTOBER
10 A.M. TO 5.30 P.M. MONDAY
TO SATURDAY
NOVEMBER TO MARCH
10 A.M. TO 4.00 P.M. TUESDAY
TO SATURDAY

We were too late. It was closed, and even the silence seemed to shut us out.

Into the emptiness came Cam's voice, as clear and tiny as a single shell on a beach.

"Is it closed?"

I didn't answer because I was thinking about how to get in. And besides, I didn't know what to say.

"Is it closed, Libby? Is it closed?"

Shut up, I thought, *I'm trying to think.* But what I said was, "I'll sort it out, Cam."

We were not going to walk meekly away. I'd told him that we'd soon be inside, and we would. We were not going to be stranded out here and the kitten was not going to die, not after all we'd been through. This was not going to happen to Cam. Never mind Cam, it wasn't going to happen to me either.

I went up to the gates and shook them hard in case I got lucky, but they didn't give way so I walked along the fence and peered through the gap between the reception hut and the surrounding trees. Then I saw what I wanted, and felt a flicker of hope like the curling leaves in the fire basket.

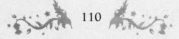

110

Beyond the reception was a row of wooden huts that looked like log cabins. In one window, a light was on. Somebody was in. I squatted down beside Cam.

"There's somebody there," I said. "Everything's locked up, but somebody's there, so we have to shout for them to let us in."

He nodded. A tear fell on to his coat.

"Oh, Cam." I hadn't realized that he was crying, and I should have done. Poor little love. I wrapped my arms round him. This had all been too much for him. All the fight was knocked out of him, and all he could do was cry and not even dry his eyes because he wouldn't let go of the tiny bump of kitten under his coat. I wiped the tears from his face.

"You're a good, brave boy," I said. "When we get home I'm going to tell my mum and your dad how brave you are. Now we have to do some shouting to make the people inside notice us. You're good at shouting. Can you do that?"

He nodded. I suspected he could barely squeak, let alone shout, but he'd feel better if he thought he was doing something useful.

"After three," I told him, "shout 'help', as loud as you can. Ready? One, two, three – HELP!"

We shouted, but our voices were too thin for that great space. I steered Cam right up to the fence and we yelled again from there. With all my strength, I rattled the gates until they clanged.

I still had the tea tray. My hands were almost too cold to grip it, but I could because I had to. I grabbed

it and swung it against those gates like a battleaxe –
CLANG, CLANG – like a school bell.

"Somebody looked!" shouted Cam. "Somebody came
to the window!"

"Wave!" I said, then realized that he couldn't, so I
ran to his side and waved. Nobody was there.

"They've gone," said Cam and kicked the snow in
anger. So did I. If it hadn't been for snow, none of
this. . . Then I remembered the wildcat springing at us
in the forest.

I scooped up a handful of snow, packed it hard, took
a few steps back, and belted it over the fence. That
first one missed, but the second one got the log cabin.
And another. Another. *Thwack. Get off your idle bum,
whoever you are, we need you. Wallop. NOW!* Cam
yelled and bellowed at the top of his voice.

A door opened and shut. A tall, lean man with short
hair was striding furiously to the gate.

"This had better be good," he said, and his accent
was sort of gentle Scots. Then Cam, with tears drying
on his face, gave a huge wet sniff and said exactly the
right thing.

"You have to save the kitten," he said.

From the gate to the long wooden hut, we stepped
shivering into another world. From outside, the hut
had just looked like a long log cabin. Inside, a wave of
warm air made me sigh with relief. It was brightly lit,
too, with a modern floor and worktops and a sink, and
everything absolutely gleaming-clean.

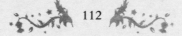

"It's like a hospital," said Cam.

"It *is* a hospital," said the man. "I'm Gordon; I'm on duty here tonight. What's this about a kitten?"

I knew Cam didn't like hospitals, but he seemed to be all right about this one. He took a good look at Gordon as if he needed to check that he could be trusted, then struggled with the collar of his jacket. My fingers were numb and clumsy, but I managed to help him with the zip and he placed the tiny kitten into Gordon's hands.

The kitten turned its head and mouthed the air. It was alive, and I knelt beside Cam and hugged him hard.

Gordon stroked the kitten's head. His eyes widened with astonishment.

"A wild kit!" he said. "Where did you find it?"

Cam started to tell him in a disjointed, confusing sort of way, and I tried to help, but something strange was happening. The warmth and all that had happened must have been getting to me, because my head felt spinny. There was a chair behind me and I sat down quickly.

"Are you all right?" asked Gordon. Still with the kitten in his hands, he opened a door. "Heather, we need some help in here!"

An older woman came in. She had a plait of greyish hair and I remember she was wearing a Fair Isle sweater that looked old and comfortable and too big for her. She took one look at us and said, "Get those wet coats off, the pair of you! Do you want to catch pneumonia?"

"Heather, we have a wildcat kitten," said Gordon

as Heather took Cam's jacket.

"We have three of them, by the look of it," remarked Heather. "What have you been doing, rolling down hills in the snow?"

Heather was just lovely, I could have hugged her. She helped us off with our boots – Cam's feet were still dry, just bright pink with cold, but she gasped in horror at my soaked socks and ditch-watery feet. All the time she was doing that, she explained things about where we were. The block we were in was partly offices and partly the hospital wing for animals in need of TLC. Somebody had brought them three orphaned fox cubs two days before and one of their own deer was hurt and needed attention. Heather was working late, and Gordon had decided his chances of getting back home through the snow that night weren't great, so he was staying put.

"You're soaked through, lassie," said Heather. "How's your hand? I'll find you some scrubs and a bag to put your wet things in. We haven't any clothes to fit the wee boy, though."

That was all right because Cam's waterproofs were a lot more waterproof than mine. He was a bit damp, but when I'd rubbed some warmth into his feet he was happy. We hadn't needed his spare socks, but I put them on a radiator so he could change into warm ones before we left. While I did that, and Heather hunted in cupboards, Cam and I managed to give the story of the dead wildcat. Then Heather showed me where the loo was (by that time I really needed it, too) and as I'd been

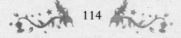

soaked to the skin she gave me a set of scrubs – those overalls that vets and doctors wear in intensive care. I felt like an extra from *Holby City*, but I was warm and dry and didn't care.

"So you carried him all that way and kept him warm, Cam?" Gordon was saying as I got back. "Good man!"

Cam turned to me with a smile so bright that I really did get tears in my eyes, but that was all right. Gordon gave the kitten back to him to hold while he took something from a freezer and put it in the microwave.

"Shall we settle him in, then?" he asked.

We followed him into a room full of cages – very big cages, all as clean as could be. At one side, in a kind of cubicle with a gate like a toddler's stair gate, was a young deer. It lay on a blanket, watching us from its deep, gentle eyes. One outstretched leg was in plaster. From a rumpled towel in a cage, a small paw showed.

"Fox cubs," remarked Gordon, nodding at the cage. He wrapped the kitten in a clean towel, popped it into a cage that looked ridiculously big for it, and washed his hands. The kitten turned its head, opening and closing its eyes. Its mouth stretched open as if it wanted to call for its mum, and it seemed to try to turn over.

The microwave pinged. Gordon took out a feeding bottle no bigger than an eye dropper and flicked a few drops of milk on to the inside of his wrist the way you check a baby's bottle.

"That'll do," he said. He lifted the scrawny little scrap of kitten and slipped the teat into its mouth.

Its eyes opened a little more. It wrapped a paw over

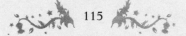

the bottle and sucked fiercely, furiously, as if it had to fight to keep this bottle, and that was when I knew it would be all right. That was when I knew we had faced the fairy-tale forest with its dark shadows, been tested by the laws of the wild lands, and come through. It was also when I stopped being able to see very well, and Heather gave me a tissue.

"Good lad!" said Gordon to the kitten. "Is that better?" Then he squatted down beside Cam. "You saved him. Do you want to feed him now? You'll need to sit down."

Without a word, Cam sat and reached out his hands for the kitten. Gordon spread a towel over his lap and helped him to angle the bottle and hold it in just the right way as it drew the warm milk into its scrap of a body. Really and truly, I could see its little belly getting rounder. It was one of the most wonderful moments of my life, ever. I would have loved to have fed the kitten myself, but even better was watching Cam so absorbed and happy. He knew he was doing something good, and he was loving it. Deep magic shone in his eyes. Soon the kitten's eyes were closing and it was slipping into a full, contented sleep. Gordon didn't attempt to take it from Cam, just left it on his lap, and Cam sat perfectly still with a calm smile on his face.

I realized that Gordon had just asked me a question. I had to get him to repeat it.

"Will anyone be worried about you two?"

I was so tired, so relieved and so glad to just sit in the warm and watch Cam feed the cat that I didn't

want to move. But this couldn't last for ever. We had to get back to the world of Mum, Gray and the cottage.

"Do you get a phone signal here?" I asked.

"It's not reliable," he said. "You can use the landline. Do you need to call your parents?"

He showed me where the office phone was and I dialled the cottage. The ringing had hardly started when it was picked up, and Mum was almost gabbling down the phone, her voice high and scared.

"Libby! Are you all right? Is Cam all right? Where are you?"

"We're where I told you," I said. "I'm at Flora's. We're fine."

I could hear Gray behind her and his voice was harsh with anxiety as he demanded to know where we were and whether we were safe. He was asking directions to Flora's so he could pick us up.

All I'd wanted, out in the snow, was to be in the cottage. Now that I was warm and dry I thought I'd much rather stay here with these kind people who knew what to do and congratulated me for what I'd done, and didn't ask me to explain anything.

Perhaps they could find a spare cage for me?

Chapter Ten

All of a sudden things didn't look so good. Mum and Gray had sounded terrified but now they knew we were safe I could imagine that terror turning to anger. I was imagining all sorts of scenes with Gray, and none of them were pretty. I went to see how Cam was getting on and found him still sitting with the kitten asleep in his lap. Heather lifted it very gently so as not to wake it up, wrapped it in the towel and put it in the cage. It looked microscopic in there, and as sweet as any other kitten. Then again, it had its eyes shut. It sneezed.

"It's caught cold!" said Cam.

"No, all cats do that," said Heather. "You kept him as snug as a bug in a rug, didn't you? You two are the ones who could catch cold. Do you like hot chocolate?"

Cam brightened up even more. Then he wanted his

jacket so he could get his black dog and hold it up to the bars of the cage so it could see the kitten. Heather brought us steaming mugs of hot chocolate.

"Is Daddy coming for us?" asked Cam with a chocolaty moustache.

"Yes, he should be here soon," I said.

"When's soon?"

"I don't know, but you'd better finish your hot chocolate first."

"I can show him the kitten," he said. "Can I stroke the deer?"

"You can't stroke her, but you can go and look at her," said Heather. "Move slowly and gently. Deer get scared easily."

"We were supposed to be coming here this morning," I said as Cam sat on the floor about a foot from the gate. "But it all went a bit. . ."

I stopped, partly because this morning felt like a week ago and also because I thought I'd better not talk about this in front of Cam. He was happy, and I didn't want to remind him of how his longed-for day at the Wildlife Centre had gone completely to pot. Then again he might not have heard us; he was already more than half in love with the deer.

"Come tomorrow," said Heather. "I'll sort out free passes for you, and what about your parents? You can see how the wee cat's doing."

"We're supposed to be going home tomorrow," I said, and I felt as if I'd walked into a brick wall. I'd been looking forward to being back home, just me and Mum

119

in our own house as usual, not having to fit in with anybody else. Normal food and my own room. Granny and Grandpa ten minutes' walk away. No more Gray to annoy me, no more being an unpaid babysitter. But I did like my room in the cottage, and the fire, and I'd quite enjoyed larking about in the snow with Cam.

I heard an engine. It could only be Gray's car.

"That must be your lift home," said Gordon, and he went to the door.

"Where's Cameron?" Harsh and loud, they were the first words I heard, and at the sound of Gray's voice Cam turned and rushed to him. It was their moment, father and son, so I stayed out of the way. I saw how Gray was white and wild-eyed as if he'd had nightmares for a week. I saw the way he folded his arms round Cam as if he could never ever ever let him go.

"Are you all right, Cam? Are you all right?" He released him just a bit, then took Cam by the shoulders, looking him up and down as if he wanted to convince himself that it really was Cam, and that he still had all his arms and legs. Then he hugged him again, hard and tight with his eyes tightly shut and his hand at the back of Cam's head, his fingers tangled in the wild dark hair. For less than a second I felt a door had opened into another world, a world with an adoring dad who was totally absorbed in this one precious child as if nothing else existed. Was that what it was like, even with useless Gray? Just for that moment, all the powers of hell couldn't have forced those two apart.

It didn't last. Cam struggled free and dragged Gray

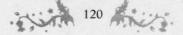

away to see the deer. Gray hadn't a clue what was going on; he stared at the animal as if he didn't know what it was, as if he'd just woken up and didn't know if he was dreaming. Then with Gray's hand in both of his, Cam pulled him to the kitten's cage. The kitten was so wrapped in a towel that you could only see its ear.

"Look!" he was saying. He managed to keep his voice low, but he couldn't help bouncing up and down. "It's a wildcat kitten and I saved it! It was going to die and we found it and I saved its life! Tell him Libby, Libby, tell him, tell him!"

"He's been fantastic," I said. "A very brave, good boy." I don't think Gray heard me.

"I saved the kitten, Dad! Libby found it and I saved it!"

"Yes, he did," I said calmly. One of us had to be. I still didn't know if any of this was getting into Gray's head. "Cam kept him warm all the way here, and saved his life. He's been a star."

"And I gave him a bottle!" Cam's voice was louder now. The deer threw up its head.

"Quiet, Cam, remember the deer," I said.

Gray seemed to notice me for the first time. At least he turned his head.

I had never seen a look like that before, or at least, not directed at me. It wasn't that he looked angry – or if it was anger, it was cold anger. It was a look that told me *if I could make you disappear from the earth for ever, I would.* Quietly and very sternly, he said, "I think we'd better go, then you can explain."

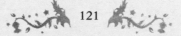

121

I folded my lips tightly and went on looking him in the eyes. What did he think I was going to do, make a meek apology after all that I'd done for Cam? I knew I'd taken a risk. I could sort of see how he felt. But I'd done it for Cam and I'd kept him safe, and now he was talking to me like that, a man I'd only met a few days ago, in front of people I liked a lot – what did he expect me to say? *I'm sorry, I've been a very naughty little girl and you are a sensible grown-up and you are right to be cross.* No, that wasn't going to happen. He wasn't going to reduce me to that. Heather and Gordon were there, they'd been kind, they'd done all the right things, and I knew they were impressed by what Cam and I had done. They understood. I wouldn't let Gray humiliate me in front of them.

"I told you where we were going," I said, very reasonably and politely. "I left a note on the table."

"We didn't see any note," he said. "And regardless, it was a hugely dangerous thing to do. We were worried sick."

Suddenly it all felt too much. I'd coped. I'd just come through blizzards, snowstorms and bitter freezing cold, and I'd done something good, and Gray had to turn up and rubbish it all. It wasn't my fault if he was too stupid to find a note on a table. I felt my face redden with anger and embarrassment.

Gordon rescued me. At least, he tried to.

"Mr. . .?" he began.

"Donaldson," said Gray.

"Mr Donaldson, I don't know what's going on here

but I do know that these two have come through a Highland white-out to bring a wildcat kitten to safety. It's the most endangered species in Scotland, and this wee thing wouldn't have stood a chance without them. And Libby has been looking after the boy all the time. If I were in danger, I'd want to be on her team. She's done everything right: she found her way here, she found shelter when they needed it. Your daughter's one in a million."

"She's not my daughter."

"I'm not his daughter."

We said it together, Gray and me, both in the same clipped and bitter way. The silence that followed was as hard and cold as mountains.

Somebody had to say something, if only for Gordon's sake. He was watching us with the air of a man who's just put his foot in his mouth and doesn't know how to get it out again.

As usual, it would have to be me. I gave Gordon the nearest I could manage to a smile.

"It's complicated," I said.

"Libby's mum's at the cottage with a broken leg," said Cam. *Thanks, Cam, that makes it all crystal clear.* "Dad, you haven't looked properly at the wild kitten!"

Gordon unwrapped the towel a bit, and Gray finally looked at the kitten. *Oh, please,* I thought, *please, whatever you think, however angry you are with me, just notice the cat, just say something nice, for Cam's sake!*

"It's a beautiful kitten," said Gray at last. "You can tell me all about it when we get home."

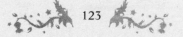

"Yes, we have to go, Cam," I said. "Let's get your boots. Your warm socks are on the radiator, and—"

I remembered that I was still in scrubs and my clothes were still making a wet puddle somewhere. I looked at Heather.

"You can drop the scrubs in when you come tomorrow," she said. Bless her, she was determined that we'd be back. I was aware of a bit of puzzlement on Gray's face as if the wet-clothes situation had outwitted him. Heather gave me a pair of those disposable slippers like plastic bags for your feet, so that stepping into my wet wellies wouldn't be as unpleasant (it was pretty unpleasant anyway, but the slippers helped), and pressed two free passes into my hand. As Gray took Cam to the car, I said quietly to Gordon, "Will the kitten be all right? It's so tiny – and it must have been away from its mum for hours."

"It should be fine," he said. "Don't you worry." Then he added kindly, "I hope everything's all right when you get back."

"It'll be fine," I said with a smile, but I think he knew I was lying. At that moment I could almost have asked Gordon and Heather to adopt me.

All the way back to the cottage, Cam sat as upright as a wide-awake cat. Nobody said a word.

Chapter Eleven

Back in the cottage in the warm light of the hall I had a moment of complete, sudden joy. If it's ever happened to you, you know exactly what I mean, and if it hasn't I don't know how to explain it — just an overwhelming sense of things being, in this moment, completely good. I knew that sooner or later Gray would go into rocket-launching mode. I wouldn't be surprised if Cam did, too. I'd had enough — I was tired, I still wasn't fully warmed through — but for a few seconds I drank in the safety of the little hallway in the cottage and everything felt right. From the sitting room came the *step-clunk*, *step-clunk* of someone walking on crutches, and Mum appeared in the doorway.

"Sweetheart, are you all right?" she cried. "We were so worried!"

I hugged her and leaned my face against her shoulder, my warm, soft, familiar mum. She smelt of clean washing. She smelt of home.

"Sit down, Mum," I said, and helped her on to the settee. "I left you a note to tell you where I was, didn't you find it?"

Determined to prove that I really had left the note, I looked at the table. Then I understood. Gray's camera was on there with some booklets from the hospital and a newspaper. When I picked them up, I saw my note underneath.

"There," I said, and I left it at that. I was too tired and, I hope, too grown-up to make a big triumph of it. Apart from anything else, I didn't want to go round in hospital scrubs for the rest of the evening. I changed into some of my own clothes and folded up the scrubs, and came back to the sitting to find Cam jumping up and down holding Mum's hands and telling her his story. He was so excited that the words got mixed up.

"We, we, we resc... We found... We, we saved a kitten!" he managed at last. "And I carried it all the way there!" Then he was rattling away about the sledge, the dead wildcat, the hut, leaping from one part of the story to another, running his words together and mixing them up – we were both so focused on him that we almost forgot about Gray until his voice, firmly raised, surprised Cam into silence.

"Cam, you're probably soaked through," he said. Cam and I both started to say that he was dry, but Gray

ignored us. "Off to our bedroom and change everything you've been wearing."

"He's OK," I said. "The waterproofs were really good."

Gray ignored me. "Quick as you can, Cam, and then we'll have the best hot chocolate ever," he said.

Cam ran off, good as gold. He seemed to take the brightness with him. Before my eyes Gray seemed to grow taller and broader, filling the space in the room, blotting out the light like a thundercloud.

"Libby, what did you think you were doing!" he demanded. "You took Cam, just the two of you, out into a blizzard with a tea tray, for goodness sake – a tea tray! You knew what the conditions were like, and you knew you couldn't get phone contact if you were lost or hurt. Did you even know the way to go?"

I opened my mouth to tell him that I'd found the way from the map and about all the stuff I'd prepared for the journey, but he didn't stop.

"Did you think for a moment what you'd do if you were trapped?"

"We—"

"Or if Cam had been injured?" His voice was louder. "Or if you'd been injured yourself, and there was nobody to help you?"

"But if—"

"Anything could have happened! You could both have been hypothermic before anyone found you. You could have collapsed with exhaustion!"

"Gray, perhaps—" began Mum, but Gray didn't seem to hear her.

127

"In all that Cam and I have been through, I have never in my life been so anxious about him!" he raged. "I've never heard anything so dangerous, so irresponsible!"

"Gray!" cried Mum, and sat up ramrod straight. "That's quite enough. Just calm down! Libby's done her best; she was left alone to cope with Cam, and they're both safe, so let's just leave it!"

I stared in astonishment. She wasn't shouting, but her straight back and angry eyes made me think of the wildcat. I had a wildcat mother! And I loved her for it.

"This is Libby's holiday too," she said firmly. "She's spent most of it looking after Cam and she's been absolutely wonderful with him, and look at him now! He's thrilled; he's full of what they've been doing! And she did tell us, Gray; she did leave that note. She was only trying to take him to Flora's because we couldn't!"

I squeezed my eyes shut and hoped nobody was looking at me.

"And has she been thanked for looking after him all week?" snapped Mum. "None of this has been easy for Libby!"

I had to rub the back of my hand across my face. Unfortunately, she noticed.

"Gray!" she exclaimed. "You've made Libby cry!"

"I wasn't crying!" I tried to say, but I could hardly get the words out.

Then I heard the tiniest sound, a snatched little gasp, from the sitting-room doorway. I looked across and saw what nobody else had seen. Cam had heard

us. He was standing just outside the open door, staring at us, shocked and close to tears. How long had he been there? Mum and Gray must have seen me looking because they both turned, saw him, and said, "Cam!" at the same time.

Cam turned and bolted for the front door. Gray ran after him and I followed as far as the hall. Cam had got past the two cars when Gray caught up with him and tried to carry him indoors, but Cam wasn't having any of it.

I was used to Cam kicking off – I had the bruises to prove it – but this time he took it to a whole new level, shrieking as if he was being murdered, kicking out with bare feet that must have been painful with cold. He got both hands into Gray's hair and pulled so hard that Gray had to put him down and hold on to his wrists.

"I'm not . . . coming . . . IN!" he screamed, and every word was drawn out long and loud as he was screaming for the stars to come down and help him. "I'm not! NOT! I HATE YOU!"

Gray ducked to avoid a headbutt and moved his arm so that Cam couldn't bite him. Something inside me was saying that this was between father and son and nothing to do with me, but I simply could not bear it. I'd spent all day trying to make Cam happy, and he *had* been happy, and I hadn't done it to end like this. And whatever I felt about Gray, I couldn't let this go on. Once again, I slipped into my wet boots.

"It's all right, Cam," I said softly. The words kind of

came to me as I went along. "You don't have to come in if you don't want to."

He stopped crying and looked up at me suspiciously. Not for the first time that day, I knelt down in the snow.

"It's just that we don't want you to get cold and wet again, that's all," I went on. "Daddy wants you to be warm by the fire with a nice drink, then maybe I can run you a bubble bath."

He hiccupped.

"Then, when you're in there, we can make some tea," I said. "Are you hungry? And if you're unhappy, you can tell us why. And you can tell Mum – Kate – everything that happened from the beginning to the end, and especially about the kitten. She wants to know all about the kitten, and how brave you were."

He thought for a few seconds, then nodded. Then he sighed so deeply that he must have sighed all the fight out of himself, and turned to the cottage.

I started his bath running and left him to Mum and Gray. Mum was on crutches, Gray needed to be with Cam, and somebody had to cook. It might help if we all sat around a table together over some sort of a hot meal, even if it was only beans on toast. Now that I thought of it, I could kill for beans on toast.

My limbs were telling me to curl up somewhere and switch off. In fact, most of me was telling me that. *Shut up and open some beans,* said my brain, so I did. I also found eggs, bacon, tomatoes, and some fruit and biscuits. Once I'd started to cook I felt less tired; in fact I became absorbed in what I was doing, sizzling the

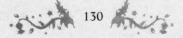

bacon and tipping the eggs into the pan. When it was nearly ready I let Mum know and went to see if Cam was out of the bath yet.

The shout of rage from the bedroom told me that, yes, Cam was out of the bath. He was having another go at Gray but at least this time he was just shouty, not hysterical. The sitting room door was open again, so Mum heard it too.

"I hate you! I hate you!" he was shouting. "You're the worst daddy ever!"

It wasn't funny. It really wasn't. I felt the giggles rising and pressed my hands to my mouth.

"Cam, listen. . ." began Gray.

"You shouted at Libby!" yelled Cam, and now there were tears in his voice. "You were horrible to Libby and you made Kate cross! You upset Kate, and now she won't like you any more and then . . . and then . . . and then . . . she won't want to be my mummy!"

Mum and I couldn't look at each other. We'd both heard that, and we couldn't unhear it now. I don't know what she did, but I went to our bedroom, shut myself in, and had a bit of a cry. What, I wondered as I aimed a tissue at the bin, what on earth were we all supposed to do now? Why did Cam's mum have to die, why did my dad leave, why were we all in such a mess?

Sometimes you just have to do the next thing, and I'd have to do it before supper was ruined. I dried my eyes, took a few deep breaths, and went back to the kitchen. The bacon was so crisp you could snap it and there was a thin baked-bean layer stuck to the bottom of the pan, but finally we were all round the table with hot food in front of us.

"Thank you, Libby," said Gray.

My mum gave my hand a quick squeeze and said, "Well done, sweetie."

Cam just said, "I love beans!" and shovelled them down. He looked exhausted, and I wasn't surprised.

Though I say it myself, it was a very nice meal, and when Cam had finished guzzling down baked beans he took a deep breath and said, "When can we go back and see the kitten?"

Oh, help. Did he never run out of steam?

"Now, tell me all about this kitten," asked Mum, and I realized that she'd still only heard disjointed bits of the story from Cam and Gray didn't know much more. So between us, Cam and I told them exactly what we'd been doing all day, and because they both had the sense to listen and not interrupt, they both got it. When we were finished they asked a few questions, but by that time poor little Cam was yawning like a pothole. Gray put him to bed while I made mugs of tea and tried not to look at the heap of dishes in the sink. Then, when Gray came back from settling Cam down, I said what had to be said.

This was my turn. I even stood up to say it, to make it clear that this was not a conversation. It was Libby's Say.

"You really need to sort this out," I said. "I didn't really mind about looking after Cam – well, I did a bit, because I don't like being taken for granted." They both

tried to speak, but I put my hand up to stop them. "Say it later. This is my turn. So I'm the one who's been with him most on this holiday, and he doesn't have a clue what's going on."

If I shouldn't have taken him out that day, I was sorry. I wouldn't have done it if he hadn't been so determined to go that he'd already tried once to set out alone. But when I first saw Cam I could see something in his eyes and I didn't know what it was. I knew now. He looked like a lost puppy, sniffing all over the place because he was looking for something familiar and safe. He was confused and afraid because all he could think of was that he wanted a nice mum, and he couldn't bear the idea that it might not happen.

"I know that Cam really wants a mum. That doesn't mean that you two have to stay together if you don't really want to. I mean, don't get married just so Cam can have a mum because if it all went wrong he'd be worse off than ever. But can't you at least have a plan? You," I turned to Gray, "I know you were worried about Cam when you came to pick him up, but you havn't paid him any attention all holiday. Even before Mum broke her leg I was looking after him because you haven't bothered with him! Whether you two stay together is up to you. I'm not going to make it harder. But just think about Cam. He's confused and misses his mum, and he needs ... needs..."

I stopped because I'd suddenly run out of knowing what to say. I'd lost the words for what Cam needed, but looking at them I could see that Gray was genuinely

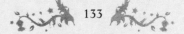

listening for once. He was really trying to understand, and I felt a bit sorry for him. Just a bit.

"I feel as if I've been the adult all weekend," I said. "I know that a lot of what happened was because of the weather, and the accident, and that none of it is anybody's fault, but it comes to the same thing. I've had to be the adult. But I don't know how to do that because I'm fourteen and I've had to make it up as I went along. So would you two please just be the adults now?"

Once I'd finished I felt as if I'd just buckle at the knees and keel over. I was tired, I was upset, and I was astonished that I'd just said all that. Was that me? And as my legs began to give way I remembered something that made me want to cry with exhaustion.

"Ailsa couldn't get down this morning," I said. "And I don't suppose she can get down now, so I'm going to get Peggy and Jayjay in."

"Libby," said Mum softly, "is it all right to talk now?" I nodded because I'd somehow forgotten how to speak. "You've done enough," she said. "Gray and I can sort out the horses."

"But you don't know what to do," I said, and I couldn't help laughing. "And your leg's in plaster!"

"Then tell me," said Gray. "I'm listening."

I didn't quite trust him to manage both of them on his own, but when we'd got outside I didn't feel so tired any more. I'd borrowed Mum's jacket and wellies because mine were still wet. What I'd said must have hit home, because Gray was like a child trying to show

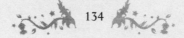

that he can be a good little boy, *Really, honestly, look, I'm doing everything just the way you say, have I got it right, Libby?* Between the two of us it didn't take long to sort out buckets and hay nets and lead them in. I nearly thanked him, and then thought better of it. When we went back inside I heard bath water running.

It was for me. Mum had run me a deep, hot bath with some of her own special bath oil. There were fresh blue bruises from Cam kicking me. I slipped down into the water and closed my eyes, reliving the day from the warmth and ease of the water. Heat seeped into me and at last the ice in my veins thawed until I was warm all the way through. I smiled. I felt loved.

I don't know what time I went to bed but it must have been stupid early. I read a bit and dozed a bit and as I did more dozing than reading I thought that we had to go home the next day, and Cam wanted to see the kitten again, and Mum couldn't drive, so how could. . .

And I stopped caring. It was somebody else's problem.

Chapter Twelve

When I woke for the first time it was because something damp was on my face. Cam was climbing in beside me with his black dog in his hand. That was the damp thing and I didn't want to think about how it had got wet. Half asleep, I pushed it away from my face, but Cam cuddled in anyway.

I was drowsing off again when he said, "Let's go and play."

"Too early."

"No, it—"

"Shut up, Cam."

He stayed very still for a while, and it was like trying to sleep beside an unexploded bomb. Finally he clambered out, pattered away round the bed and got into Mum's bed instead. If this relationship was going to last Cam would need an alarm clock and strict instructions about not waking anybody up before it rang. That was my last thought before I drifted off again.

I woke for the second time to hear Gray's voice in the hall, and then Cam was standing beside me with a big smile and a mug of tea. I half sat up and managed a sleepy smile and a thank you, then looked past him at Gray, who was bringing tea to Mum. He looked different. He looked like a proper, sensible dad, knowing what he had to do and getting on with it. (Fortunately the carpet had one of those mixed patterns that doesn't show if you drip tea on it.) By the time Mum and I were dressed – I had to help Mum – Gray had sorted breakfast and we sat down together to talk about the when, where and how of the day.

"We have to get to Flora's for Cam's special day, don't we, Cam?" said Mum.

Cam nodded enthusiastically with his mouth full.

"I've been to see Ailsa," said Gray. "If we're going to Flora's we can't get home today, so I needed to sort out an extra night. She was fine with it."

I'd begun to look forward to my own home and my own bed, and I'd planned on going over to Granny and Grandpa's the next day because I had so much I wanted to talk over with them. Still, one more night was one more night in that cute little room, and Gray was trying to be reasonable. He was right about taking a whole day at Flora's. Cam was soon badgering

Mum to read him a story, so I left them to it and went to wash up. Gray came too, and helped.

"Cam told me about the bothy," he said, putting the butter in the fridge.

"The what?" I asked.

"The bothy – the hut where you sheltered. That's what they're called. Cam said he really liked it because he had his biscuits and a drink in there and you wrapped your coat round him. He said it was like a kangaroo picnic."

That made me laugh. "I'm glad he enjoyed it," I said.

"What I mean to say," Gray went on, "is that Libby, I'm sorry for the way I behaved yesterday. I was completely unjust to you."

Oh. I could have said that it was all right, and we could forget it. But I would have been lying because it didn't feel all right, not yet. So I said nothing, just gave him the teapot to dry.

When we got here I'd been desperate for a break," he said. "Between work and Cam I was exhausted. I know you think I'm a rotten father."

I'd been thinking that all weekend, he didn't have to be a mind reader to work it out. But now I wasn't so sure, so I still said nothing.

"I probably am," he said. *Really?* "Cam's exhausting and it's always harder at this time of year – it's too dark to do stuff after work. I probably let him spend too much time in front of a screen. Getting here was a long drive and he was stressing for every inch of it: *What will it be like, what's Kate like, what's Libby like, when*

138

will we get there? Every time he saw a service station he said he needed a wee. Every time we saw a cottage he asked if it was the right one, then after darkness fell and we were on the little winding roads he kept wailing that we must be lost. Cam doesn't have an off switch. By the time we got here I was desperate to zone out, and Cam sort of wrapped himself round you and Kate and you were both so good with him. I shouldn't have left you so much to get on with it, though, and I'm sorry about that."

I shrugged and let him go on.

"Neither of us were happy about leaving you here alone when Kate was in hospital," he said. "And after we'd been snowbound all night I wanted to leave early in the morning, but we had to wait until Kate had seen the consultant. When we finally did get away the traffic was crawling. I could have pushed her home on a hospital trolley faster, and all the time I was dying to just scoop Cam up and hug him."

I sort of nodded to show that I'd heard, and wrung out a cloth hard to clean the sink. Finally, still looking at the sink, I said, "I really am sorry about yesterday," because it was true. It had turned out all right, it had been an adventure, no harm had come to either of us. But I hadn't allowed for a Highland winter, how suddenly and viciously the weather could change. I finished the sink – I'd nearly scrubbed a hole in it – and found the dustpan and brush so I could sweep the floor.

"Cam wanted to go so much," I said. "I tried to

explain to him about not going, but he didn't seem to get it."

I could hear the grin on Gray's face. "Cam has that effect on people," he said. "Now that I've talked to him I don't think he was ever afraid. I just panicked, Libby. We got home and called for you both. There was silence. I didn't worry at first; I went to see if you were outside, sledging on the tea tray or something. But I couldn't see you, time went on, I had no idea where you were – honestly, I was scared." There was a pause, then he added, almost as if he didn't want to say it, "There are times when I feel, if anything goes wrong for Cam, I'm letting his mum down."

The smile had gone out of his voice now. He was standing with his back against the kitchen bench, leaning his hands on it, looking at the floor. I didn't know what to say, so I hung up the dustpan and brush and looked for something else to clean. There wasn't anything, so I shuffled the washing around on the radiator.

Gray loved Cam. He didn't always show it in the way I thought he should, but I'd seen the way he hugged him the day before. I could see it now, too, as he talked about how frightened he'd been, not knowing where Cam was. Cam was his world, the way Mum and I were each other's world. And I was old enough to sort myself out, but Cam was only six. How does that feel, coming home expecting to find your six-year-old safe in a warm house and finding that he's not there? Nobody's there, and your little boy's out there in that vast icy

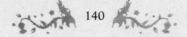

140

wilderness. What does that do to you? Does your stomach tie in a knot, do you shake, do you imagine the worst?

Gently, I said, "It must be really hard." It didn't say half of what I meant, but it was all I could think of.

He smiled. "We get by," he said. "I'd better go and see what he's up to. Your mum might need rescuing."

"Gray," I said, and it took me a huge effort, a real dragging-it-out-of-me effort, but it had to be said, "it's all right. I mean, you seeing my mum. I'm OK with it."

Ailsa came down to let Peggy and Jayjay out, and said the main roads were clear and we'd have no trouble getting to some shops. The local roads were still a bit scary, so it was a good thing that Gray drove that posh tractor thing. When Cam saw Ailsa he came pelting out to help with the horses, and then he had to tell Ailsa all about the kitten – he was so excited that the words were coming out of his mouth in the wrong order and I don't suppose Ailsa understood more than half of them, but then Gray appeared and rescued her.

"If we're going to Flora's you'd better get ready," he said, and Cam gave a roar of excitement and charged into the house. Then we all laughed, Ailsa, Gray, me and Mum who was at the window, and I realized that it was the first time we'd all laughed together. It felt good. I wanted more.

"What's happening about getting home again

tomorrow, though?" I asked as we followed Gray indoors.

"All sorted," said Gray without looking at me. "Your mum has a great insurance policy."

So that had been sorted, then. Now all I had to worry about was whether the kitten had survived the night. *Please, please, please.*

Arriving at Flora's couldn't have been more different from the day before. It was daylight, everything was open, and the place was alive. There were families there, excited kids getting out of cars with their little backpacks, babies in carriers, grandparents drinking coffee out of flasks. Cam ran to the ticket office with Gray hurrying after him to stop him from pushing ahead in the queue, and I followed with Mum – *clunk and a step, clunk and a step.* Gray was at the front of the queue when we caught up.

"There was a wildcat kitten brought in last night," he began, "do you know if it's—"

Cam popped up beside him. Even on tiptoe, he could barely see over the counter. I'd given him his free pass and he held it up in his hot sticky little hand. "We've come to see the kitten!" he announced.

"Oh!" said the girl at the office. It was as if he'd cast a spell on her. "Are you Cam! Can you wait a moment, please?" She reached for a mobile phone and simply said, "Cam Donaldson's here!"

We soon found out that everyone at Flora's had heard about the Great Kitten Rescue. In no time,

Gordon was striding out to meet us. Cam ran to him.

"Hi, Cam!" he called with a big grin. "High five! Libby! How are you doing? Hello, er. . ."

"Gray. We met last night, and this is Kate, Libby's mum," said Gray, which meant that Gordon could work out for himself what this not-family situation was. I wanted to tell him that it was OK, Gray had calmed down and wouldn't bite him, but I think he'd worked that one out too. And from the look on his face, I knew I could stop worrying about the kitten.

"Do you want to come and see Camcat?" he asked.

"Camcat!" repeated Cam.

"We named him after you, Cam," said Gordon.

"After me!" Cam took a deep breath and I could see he was gathering strength for one of those shouts that would break glass. All at the same time, Mum, Gray and I put a finger to our lips and went, "Shh!"

Cam let out the breath slowly. It turned white in front of him.

"Camcat!" he whispered with pride.

We were all ushered along to that Little House in the Big Woods place where we'd been the night before. It was different by day, full of busy people, and I noticed the sharp, clean smell along with another not so sharp, clean smell because the deer had just pooed on the floor. It felt like a different world. We seemed to have a different Gray, too. And a different me?

Gordon reached into the cage that looked so

enormous and brought out that tiny scrap of kitten, lying curled up like a hairy caterpillar in his big hand.

"Oh, bless his little bum!" exclaimed Mum, and Gray went a bit gooey too. (This was not the time to tell them it would grow up to be a mad-eyed killer.) Cam just smiled with adoration.

"Sit down, Cam, and you can hold him," said Gordon. Cam sat down on the nearest chair and cupped his hands, and Gordon lowered the kitten very gently into the little pink palms. It blinked, showing yellow-green eyes. It was such a baby thing, lying on its side with its soft paws stretched out, so absorbed in its sleep. It was less than twenty-four hours since we'd brought it in, but it looked a lot healthier than when we'd found it. It seemed fatter.

"He looks better already," I said.

"He should," said Gordon. "He's been fed every two hours through the night."

The striped tail twitched, and the kitten rolled over on to its front. It flexed its claws, and Gordon scooped it up.

"You needn't dig your claws into Cam, after all he's done for you," he said, and he returned the kitten to its cage. Cam wanted to know if he could feed it again, but Gordon said it had just been fed.

"But if you're here for the day, you can feed him later," said Gordon. "Come here at about" – he glanced at the clock – "about twelve thirty. He'll be hungry again by then. If I'm not here, Heather will be around."

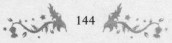

Heather had come in while we were talking, and she wasn't the only one. Quietly, since we'd arrived, the room had filled up. At first I assumed that they'd come to see the kitten, but they were the staff, they could see him any time. They'd come to see us – well, Cam, anyway. I thought of the long, quiet night, with Gordon and Heather taking turns, sleeping and feeding the kitten. Did these people ever go home?

"The most important thing you did was keeping him warm, Cam," said Heather. "He wouldn't have survived much longer outside."

Somebody else asked about exactly where we'd found him, and then there was another question, and I ended up telling the whole story again. Cam had gone to see the deer and didn't interrupt much, which saved a lot of time and confusion. When I got to the bit about sheltering in the bothy, Cam joined in without taking his eyes off the deer.

"It wasn't very much cold," he said. "Not like Libby says."

"It was freezing!" I said.

I wasn't very much cold," he said again. "Just my face and my feet. We did kangaroos."

Gray put his hand on my shoulder for a moment like a thank you, a "well done". He knew that I was the reason Cam hadn't felt so cold. It felt like a "dad" moment.

"Shall we go and see all the other animals, Cam?" suggested Gray. If he hadn't said that we would have had to drag Cam bodily away from that deer. And soon

145

we were outside, with Cam running ahead through the snow, finally having the day out he'd wanted so much, scampering about like a puppy in a field of rabbits – look what I've found, ooh, what's this, oh look, here's something else! He stopped suddenly and yelled, "REINDEER!" and a herd of little horses stampeded. After that we repeated the conversation about How Not To Frighten The Animals and he calmed down a bit.

He thought the reindeer were wonderful. So did I. They looked strong, patient and craggy, and there were elk (or is it elks?) with big kind, ugly faces. They must have been used to people wandering about because they didn't mind visitors hanging over fences to look at them.

Deer are normally shy, but the ones here weren't. They just turned their heads to look at us and decided we weren't worth bothering with. There was an aviary block, too, or at least, an owlery. There's something a bit sinister about owls – their beaks look so cruel, and they have a severe way of looking at you. (I had a maths teacher who looked like an owl, except that she couldn't turn her head right round like that. At least, she never did it when I was watching.) So I wasn't that keen to see the owls, but I went in because Cam was hanging on to my hand. We weren't in there long, and soon he found something else to get excited about.

"Are those weasels?" he asked.

"They're pine martens," I said. Gray said it at the same time, but he only knew because he was

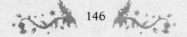

reading it from the notice on the fence. The pine martens were sweet, though, chasing each other in and out of drainpipes and rolling over. Cam was fascinated. Mum's favourite thing was the Arctic fox. As Gray pointed out, it didn't do anything, just sat there looking foxy, but she said it was beautiful. I wondered if Flora's might adopt Gray's hat. Of course Mum had to photograph everything, so I thought we'd never get round. To handle the camera she had to give me her crutch and Gray would hold her up, or she'd lean on a fence. At least she couldn't do that crouching down thing that photographers do, or we'd still be there.

I left her to it and went to lean on a fence and look at the wild horses. Wild, yes, but small and rather cute with short necks. Then Mum had to stop photographing things because I told her I wouldn't give her the crutch back until she put the camera away, and she offered to feed me to the wolves. Oh yes, they had wolves, too. And we saw a full-grown wildcat which I'm glad to say was in an enclosure. As it scowled down at us, Cam told the guy on duty about rescuing Camcat, and once again we were the famous Cam and Libby. Then Cam asked him that question that he'd asked me in the forest, but he obviously wasn't satisfied with my answer.

"Why don't the daddy animals look after the children?"

"Some do," said the guy, "but some daddy animals aren't very good at looking after the young. They go

147

away and leave the mummies to do it."

"That's what Libby's dad did," said Cam.

Thanks, Cam! Just in case I forgot what an annoying. . . It was rather Too Much Information for the poor guy looking after the wolves, and there was an awkward silence before Mum pointed out that we'd better turn back now to get Cam to the hospital for kitten feeding time. Gray and Cam went on ahead, with Mum and me lurching along behind. I wanted to know more about Gray and Cam.

"Is it just Gray and Cam?" I asked. "Are there any other family?"

"Gray's family are a long way away," Mum said. "And Fran's parents – Cam's mum's parents – sometimes come over, but it's a bit awkward."

"Don't they get on with Gray?"

"It's not that," she said. I glanced sideways and saw that she was looking down at the snow and frowning a bit. "They're lovely. . ." she paused again.

"But?" I put in, because there obviously was a "but".

". . . they used to look after Cam when Gray was at work, but they felt that he'd had enough trouble for one short life, so they spoilt him rotten. Cam knew that he just had to cry or shout to get what he wanted and do what he liked. When Gray said that he was going to employ a childminder instead they were very upset, but it had to be done. Cam can still be tempestuous now, but he's come on a lot since then. And Gray's relationships with his in-laws are improving."

So the Cam I knew was the improved version? I felt

a bit sorry for Gray.

"So," I said, "when he kicks off and everything, is that just because he's been spoilt?".

"Maybe," she said. "And he's still dealing with losing his mum. He's a complicated little soul."

"Funny little Cam," I said.

"I was going to say, he's hard work," said Mum. "When I first met Gray he hadn't had a decent night's sleep for a year. Cam was like living with a volcano and you never knew when he'd explode."

I looked ahead at Cam and Gray walking together. They'd been through a lot, the pair of them. And Gray had done all right. He was still a bit useless, but not quite as useless as I'd thought.

"When they got to the cottage and you took Cam under your wing, Gray thought all his birthdays had come at once," she said. "I've never seen him so relaxed. He hadn't had a break in so long. And he hasn't been skiing for ages. He really was grateful – but maybe we got a bit carried away. And yesterday. . ."

"Gray and I have had that conversation, Mum," I said. "It's OK." It was getting a bit embarrassing in a way, so I tried to think of something to say to change the subject. I tried hard. Nothing came to mind. *Nothing*. Something highly perceptive and intelligent. *Definitely nothing*. Or something witty. *Nothing-nothing*. Even something sensible would do. *Abso-nothing-lutely nothingy nothingy nothing*.

"I suppose most of us just want everyone to be happy," I muttered. "But we don't always know how to do it." Then to my great relief, something cute ran up a tree.

"Look, Mum!" I said. "Red squirrel!"

In the hospital block, we all watched while Cam sat on a bench with a towel on his lap and fed the kitten from its eye-dropper bottle. He was so devoted, so focused, that we all became very quiet and still as if we were sitting in a church and didn't want to interrupt the prayers. Then Gray said gently, "Cam, do you think Libby might like to feed him?"

I felt myself turn pink and my stomach did a flip. Surely it didn't show on my face? Surely nobody could tell that I would love to feed the kitten? Oh, but I would, I so would. I was going to say, "no, it's all right," because I didn't want to spoil the magic for Cam, but he just looked up and sort of shuffled over on the bench. Most carefully, he slipped a hand under the towel and passed the kitten into my lap.

"You hold the bottle like this," he said solemnly. "You keep it up that way."

I could feel the strong sucking of the tiny jaws and I smiled, not just because it was so sweet, but because there was something funny about all this tender loving care for something that would grow into a ruthless killer. *I am nourishing a wildcat, and that's bad news if you're a vole.* Then I remembered that the wild places have their own rules, not mine.

I didn't hold the kitten for long. It had been lovely of Cam to hand it over, and I didn't want to keep it from

him.

"You do it better than I do," I said as I handed it back.

Cam smiled down at the kitten. "He knows me," he said. He thought for a moment, then said, "if it was a little girl it would be Libbycat." He looked up at Gordon. "Does he have to go to bed now?"

"Soon," said Gordon, smiling.

Cam nodded solemnly, then lifted the kitten to his face and laid his cheek against the top of its head. His eyes closed and he stayed absolutely still in a moment that was only for him and the kitten, as if a bubble surrounded them. And yet . . . and yet, in another way it wasn't just Cam and the kitten. In some way it was Cam and his mum, Cam and my mum, Cam and Gray, all those loves that he needed so much. With a twist of my heart, I saw that it was Cam and me.

He kissed it, passed it back to Gordon, then took Gray's hand.

"Good boy," said Gray. "Now that the kitten's had his lunch, I think we should have ours."

The cafe was in an upstairs room with lots of windows, so we could see the squirrels twirling their lovely tails as they chased each other through the treetops and raided the bird feeders. It was almost like being in a tree house. We just had toasties, but it was fun having a meal that none of us had cooked and none of us had to wash up. That would come later, but I wasn't going to think about it yet. I think it was the first time that

holiday that I'd felt completely relaxed, worry-free and happy. I wasn't feeling grumpy about Gray and Cam wasn't having hysterics. He was even staying on his chair at the table, and if he did start anything it was Gray's problem, not mine. Gordon came over to talk to us.

"I don't know how you'll feel about this," he said, "but I'm thinking that the local paper would love to do something about you rescuing the kitten. It would be a great story and they'd want a photograph. What do you think?"

Cam just shrugged. I was about to say I was fine with it when Gray said, "I'm not sure about Cam's picture in the paper. Even if it's just the local paper, stories like that have a way of going viral these days. I wouldn't want Cam to become some kind of overnight celebrity."

I heard the gentle flapping of wings as a pig soared overhead. Gray had said something far-sighted and sensible. (And a bit Mother Wildcat-ish, too.) It might have been a bit of an overreaction, but I could understand it.

Gordon understood, too, and asked if they could just put something in their own newsletter about it with a photo of the kitten, not us, and just having our names. Gray was OK about that, and while all this was happening I could see Cam wriggling his chair closer to Mum's until he was leaning against her shoulder and looking up at her with a faraway, contented look on his face. Gray saw it, too. He turned quickly and looked

out of the window as if he absolutely had to stare at the squirrels without being interrupted.

Overwhelmed. That was the word. He'd seen Cam cuddling up to Mum with such adoration and he was overwhelmed.

We'd been through so much. And now it came to this, sitting round a table like a real family, except that no six-year-old would normally gaze at his mum like that. Children take their mums for granted. Cam couldn't do that.

When Gray had finished staring at squirrels we had cake and more drinks, and talked about what there still was to see in the Wildlife Centre. We hadn't been to the exhibition yet, and there was some hands-on stuff that Cam would like. So off we went again, seeing more animals, doing the puzzles in the exhibition, and while we did, Mum and Gray glanced at their watches, and I saw them shoot each other a little glance.

"Do we have to go soon?" I asked. We'd have to allow time for Cam to say goodbye to the cat, (and the rest of his favourite animals), and we still had to shop for the evening meal. I was wondering if there was a chippy within a couple of hundred miles.

"No, no," said Mum airily.

"It's fine," said Gray.

"Only we still have to get dinner," I said. It was a pity to remind them when everyone was having such a nice time, but perhaps I needed to be The Sensible One again.

"We're on it," said Gray.

153

"It's all sorted," said Mum. "Go and enjoy yourself!"

There was a play park corner with slides and swings and things, and Gray took Cam in there. I sat in the Visitor Centre and watched a film about otters, and Mum went off somewhere. When the film was finished I wandered out to see where everyone had got to.

I stared. My heart did a somersaulty thing. Such familiar faces in a strange place. I ran and hurled myself into my Grandpa's arms.

Chapter Thirteen

When I'd finished squishing Grandpa I squished Granny and stood back to look at her wise, smiling face. She smelt of lily-of-the-valley perfume. Home had come into my life again, making it better and stronger and wonderfully happy. If Granny had magicked up a kettle, a teapot and a plate of scones I wouldn't have been surprised.

"How are you here?" I said.

"Gray phoned us," said Granny. "Your Mum didn't tell you; she thought we'd be a nice surprise."

"Rubbish surprise, if you ask me," said Grandpa.

"Be quiet, Richard," said Granny. "Gray rang from the hospital the other day and again from Ailsa's early this morning. We booked ourselves into a hotel near the ski slopes and came up. What a marvellous place this is! If we'd known the Highlands were like this we would have come here years ago."

"So. . ." my brain was trying to catch up, "so, are you here to take us home?"

Yes, that was the idea. Granny and Grandpa would stay overnight at their hotel and in the morning they'd drive to the cottage. Grandpa would drive their car home and Granny would drive Mum's because she's on Mum's insurance. They'd sorted it all out without needing me to do a thing about it.

We took them to the play-park, where they met Gray and Cam and I willed Cam to behave. He'd just been up the scramble netting, over the wobbly bridge and down the tube slide, so he was tousled, a bit dirty, and as hyper as a puppy on espresso. When he was introduced he tipped back his head to look up at Grandpa.

"I saved a wildcat kitten and they're very rare!" It wasn't exactly a shout, but it wasn't far off.

I flinched. But Grandpa just sat down on a swing and said, "That's exciting! Tell me all about it!"

Cam would have told him all about it anyway, but it was nice that Grandpa had asked. Cam was ready to tell him about every footstep, every squirrel and every single snowflake – twice – but we managed to hurry him on before Grandpa's poor old bum could freeze to the swing. Mum didn't feel up to another *step-clunk* all the way round the enclosures, so she went to cuddle a cup of tea in the cafe and I went round again with Granny and Grandpa, Gray and Cam. Cam ran ahead,

stopping for us to catch up so he could talk about the holiday, the sledge, the ski slopes and the wildcat, not necessarily in that order. Not necessarily in any order. Half the time I didn't know what he was talking about and I'd been there. One minute he was marching through the snow describing building a snowman and the next he was giving Granny and Grandpa a lecture about the unpleasant habits of wolves. I knew him well enough by now to know what he was really doing. He was desperately showing off to Granny and Grandpa, wanting attention, wanting to impress this new *might-be* extended family. A few times Gray hushed him so that somebody else could get a word in.

"He's just overexcited," I said quietly to Granny.

She just smiled her calm smile. "I know," she said. "He'll settle down."

Eventually he did, and shut up for long enough to listen while Granny told him about a deer that used to come into their garden. In time we got on to the orphan otter that they took in, too, and the lame fox. (I remembered the fox, but the otter was before I was born.)

"At your house?" asked Cam, and I knew he was about to invite himself.

"Yes, at our house," said Grandpa.

"Do Libby and Kate live there?"

"No," said Granny. "Just the two of us, and Poppy the dog."

"Poppy the dog?" repeated Cam, and I knew what was coming next. "Can I come to your house?"

"Don't invite yourself, Cam!" said Gray, but Granny and Grandpa just laughed.

"We'll see," said Granny. Cam ran ahead, fell on his bottom again, started to roar, then suddenly stopped, stood up, and dusted himself off. The roar must have been half out of his mouth when he remembered that he was trying to impress people.

"Do you want to come and see our cottage?" he asked.

"We'll see it in the morning," said Granny. "We're coming to take Kate and Libby home."

"You can come tonight if you like," offered Cam airily. "You can come and have tea and Libby can light the fire. It's a proper fire."

"That's very kind," said Granny, "but we thought you might like to have dinner – tea – whatever it is, with us this evening."

"Oh, Granny!" I said. The day just got even better. *Yes!*

We stayed at Flora's until it closed, by which time I'd sneaked back to the cafe with Mum. Enough was enough – it had been a long day and I'd been Cammed to death. Of course Granny and Grandpa had to be introduced to Camcat who even bothered to open his eyes and take a good look at us. And as Grandpa heard the story again and talked to Gordon I knew that he was pleased – he was proud of me – and that made my heart warm.

Mum and Gray slipped me some money to treat

myself and told Cam he could choose something from the gift shop. They had the usual range of cuddly animals (I bought a little white Arctic fox) and he looked for a wildcat. Strangely enough, they didn't have one. That's odd, when you think about it, because you can get all kinds of scary people-eaters in cuddly toys, lion cubs and tigers, cute cuddly crocodiles, alligators, rhinos, everything with teeth, claws and disgusting habits. But even at Flora's we couldn't buy a cuddly wildcat. Nobody could make one of those things cute. After a lot of picking things up and putting them down again Cam finally decided he wanted a Highland cow, or a Hielan' coo as they're known locally. It was squirrel red and shaggy with hair over its eyes and handlebar horns, and he called it Libby. It wasn't the first time he'd compared me to a cow, but this time he meant it in a good way. At least I hope he did.

Mum and Cam went in Gray's car, and I was with Granny and Grandpa. It was getting dark, but I recognized the road. It was the way we'd gone to the ski slope. That area was quite touristy so I reckoned there must be a lot of restaurants.

As we drove on and darkness gathered, lights appeared in the hills around us. Local people were coming home from work and visitors were returning to their hotels like birds homing to their nests. Lights came on in houses up and down the hillsides. Granny said what I was thinking: "It's like driving in fairyland!"

"I hope the fairies have got their thermals on or

they'll catch their deaths," observed Grandpa, and I said that it was like driving in the sky, because the stars wouldn't mind the cold. I saw the sign to the ski slope, and I was a bit puzzled when Grandpa turned off there because as far as I remembered it didn't go anywhere else. Grandpa drove into the car park.

"Isn't this all shut now?" I asked.

"There's a restaurant in the Eyrie that's open in the evenings," said Grandpa. "We looked at the website; they open it late in school holidays and keep the train running. We booked a table."

The train carried us up to the Eyrie with Cam pressing his nose, his black dog and the new Coo up to the window all the way there, his mouth open as if he wanted to drink down the night sky. Then we were in the Eyrie, warm and modern and brightly lit, and looking as if we could step out of the windows and into the snow and stars.

For a moment, nobody said anything. It was too powerful, too beautiful, too far beyond the ordinary. Then somebody came and led us to a table by the window and Cam showed Grandpa where the jigsaws were. The food wasn't posh restaurant food; it was simple, hot and comforting. They even had chips, and I'd been *dying* for chips.

I sat back and looked round us. How did this happen? We were eating, talking and laughing, we were warm and fed; we were family. Whatever happened in the future, for this evening, we were family.

Cam leaned across the table to me and said, at

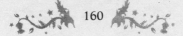

his usual volume, "What do I call your Granny and Grandpa?"

"You'll have to ask them," I told him, and Granny just said:

"Granny Josie and Grandpa Richard."

I could have hugged her.

At last Granny and Grandpa went back to their hotel and we drove to the cottage. I wanted to lie in bed and read/drink hot chocolate/look round at the snow. No chance. I switched off like a power cut and woke up knowing that it really was time to move on. The holiday had run its course and the cottage was politely explaining to me that it was time to leave it alone. I was all packed before breakfast, and by the time Granny and Grandpa arrived we were ready to go. Cam wanted to introduce Granny and Grandpa to Peggy and Jayjay, and I went with them so that Mum and Gray could have some time to themselves.

It wasn't an easy parting, not with Cam following Mum everywhere with tears brimming in his eyes. At the end I think we all expected him to make a scene, but he just clung on to her, pale and quiet. Poor little thing. She promised that they could come to our house soon and finally he curled up in the car with his Black Dog and his Libby Coo, his head down, refusing to look at anyone. Poor, funny, odd little Cam. I wanted so much to wrap him in my arms and hug him.

All the way back through the little roads I was watching for traces of green through the snow, and when the time came for us to take one turning and Gray and Cam to take the other, I waved, and saw Cam pressing Black Dog and his Highland cow against the window.

From then on, I wanted us to stay together. I didn't know if it would happen – it depended on Mum and Gray. And if it did work out Mum and I would have to cope with Cam, not just for a few days, but twenty-four seven, in his sweet times and in his furies.

What would the mother wildcat have done? I supposed she'd keep her wild kittens in order and put them firmly back in their place if they tried to step out of line, then at six months or so they'd go off and look after themselves. But a Cam is for life. And I remembered that desperate, tearful cry – "*now she won't like you any more and she won't be my mummy!*"

"Are you all right?" asked Granny.

"Sure," I muttered, and I looked out of the window.

Chapter Fourteen

That was more than a year ago. Over that year we've all lost a few sharp corners so that we fit better together.

Gray and Mum are still together and I'm pretty sure they'll last. Mum sometimes talks vaguely about "when we need a bigger house", and "if circumstances change", and it seems to be a case of when, not if. I found she'd bookmarked an estate agent's site and a wedding site on the computer, and I hope that they do get married. It would be a secure thing to do, making it official and real. And I'd happily be a bridesmaid so long as I don't have to wear pink.

Gray can still be a total idiot – he gets bright ideas and wants us all to join in with them. His last bright notion was for us all to have a narrowboat holiday. A week on a boat the size of a bathtub, moving very slowly on filthy water. With Cam. What could possibly go wrong? "That may not be a good idea," Mum had said, and I'd said, "What part of 'no, no, never-ever-ever in the world' don't you understand?" He's surprisingly teachable, but he still slides down mountains. And they say Cam's the one with problems. But Gray's OK really. Still a bit clueless, but OK. Back in the cottage we got off to a bad start, but we get on all right now. Looking back, I'd set a high standard and I think I wanted him to fail. And it can be fun having an idiot around. He takes Cam geocaching; they make a big "dad and lad" thing of it. And he's an amazing cook. We don't always know exactly what we're eating, but it's always good.

He still wears his stupid cat hat, but only in winter. At Christmas I put it on the floor and gave it a saucer of milk. He makes Mum happy, and that's the important thing.

We've had them both to stay lots, and once when Gray was away sliding down mountains we had Cam here on his own. He was so good I thought Gray must have taken his batteries out. And he absolutely adores Granny and Grandpa. We go there and take Poppy for long walks, feed the horses, and look out for hedgehogs. When we're out he's either running ahead or holding Granny's hand. They are simply brilliant with him. He's seeing some doctors to get help with managing his anger. We're all learning. It's a bit embarrassing in a way, remembering that last year I thought I was the expert on parenting. Now I'm only an expert on Cam.

He's *our* little Cam. Oh, and I'm getting to be an expert on hedgehogs and rabbits too. I help at the place where Grandpa volunteers.

THE LIBBY SUTTON
GOOD ENOUGH GUIDE TO FAMILIES

All families have their problems, even the ones with a mum and a day, a little boy, a little girl, and a poodle. Family fallouts are normal. What matters is what you do about them.

Give each other time.

Decide which issues are worth making a fuss about.

Think before you open your mouth.

Remember, other people have struggles that you don't know about.

Laugh about stuff together.

Heather keeps us up to date with Camcat and sends photographs. He's now living in the wild, but they're tracking him and Cam has pictures of him all over his bedroom.

I sent Ailsa a card to say how much I'd enjoyed staying at her cottage and to thank her for all the trouble she'd taken over us. I sent a present, too. A tea tray. I reckoned she'd need a new one.

I'm checking out the local schools, too, for Cam. From what Mum's said, if they get married, and they probably will, it'll be a case of Gray and Cam moving here, not the other way round (I should think so too, we need to stay close to my grandparents.) My old primary school was OK when I was there, but it's a bit rough and tumble and it might not be right for Cam. He needs somewhere that he'll be accepted, and they can cope with his needs, with an excellent anti-bullying policy that really works and a really lovely head. And I'll keep an eye on things. Oh, yes. Nobody, but nobody, will pick on my little br—

. . . on our Cam.

Look out for more by
Margi McAllister

When Master Ted goes to fight at the outbreak
of World War One, it falls to Archie to look after Star.

Archie has always thought Star was a complete
nuisance, but before Archie knows it, an unbreakable
bond has grown between them. And soon Archie and
his dog go on an adventure like no other...

Margi McAllister

THE
SUMMER
LION

Nothing is more powerful than friendship

Lullwater Lake is the perfect place
to spend the summer.

But this year Drina arrives to find it changed.
A sinister businessman has bought
the nearby castle, fenced off the lake and
is about to start building a vast holiday resort.

Worst of all he has his sights
set on Drina's beloved rescue lion...